THE CITADEL

BOOK THREE IN THE ZOMBIE UPRISING SERIES

M.A. ROBBINS

To F. Gary Newton, Simon of Simon's Sanctorum. He made late night horror movies fun for a teenager in the early 70's.

1

————

The Cessna flew smoothly beneath the blue Washington sky. Jen looked around at her fellow bedraggled passengers. Finding out Seattle was a dead city had taken the wind out of all of them. *That and almost getting wasted at Klawock. Took two damn weeks to get out of there.*

Grant moved in the back, sending a breeze of body odor in her direction.

"Damn," she said. "Want to keep your funk back there? You'd knock out a zombie at a hundred yards."

Grant scowled. "You don't exactly smell like sugar and spice."

Jen ignored him. They'd been stuck in close quarters for so long, it was no wonder they were snapping at each other.

She watched out the window. *Haven't seen a moving vehicle in the past hour. Lots of ant people, but they all stumbled around.*

"Fifteen miles out," Mark said. "Time to try and raise someone." He reached for the mic and keyed it. "Fairchild Control, this is N400204. Do you read?"

The radio remained quiet.

"They're probably all dead, too," Grant said.

"Tell us what you really think, Eeyore." Jen caught Mark's eye. "Took less than two weeks for that crud to get down here and take out Seattle. Wonder how far it's gone?"

"For all we know, it's everywhere." Mark raised the mic. "Fairchild Tower, do you read? This is N400204. Come in."

Zeke sat in the back, reading a manga he'd somehow stashed in his ninja costume. He looked up. "What do we do if they don't answer?"

Mark sighed. "Guess we'll fly by and see what's going on. If it looks clear, we can land and forage. They're bound to have fuel, just hoping it isn't all jet fuel."

"N400204, this is Fairchild Control. Can barely hear you through the static. What's your location?"

Mark straightened in his seat. "About fifteen miles due west of your position."

"N400204. Repeat."

"Piece of shit radio." Jen hit it with her open fist.

"Fairchild Control," Mark said, "our location is approximately fifteen miles due west of your position."

"Roger, N400204. You are ordered to change course. There is a ten-mile no-fly zone around our location."

"Negative, Control," Mark said. "Your location is our destination."

The radio remained quiet.

"Fairchild Control," Mark said. "Your location is our destination. Do you read?"

"You are ordered to change course, N400204. There is a ten-mile no-fly zone around my location."

Mark looked at the others. "Can you believe this shit?"

Jen put out her hand. "Let me try."

Grant put a hand over his face. "This never turns out good."

Mark handed her the mic and she made a face at Grant. She keyed the mic. "Fairchild Control. This is N400204. We've flown all the way from Anchorage. We're running out of fuel and need to land at your location. Do you read?"

"N400204. Did you say Anchorage? Confirm."

"Yes. Roger. Affirmative. Whatever the right word is."

"Change your heading, N400204, or you'll be shot down."

Zeke looked up from his manga, a hoop earring swinging from his ear. "He sounds serious. Do you think he'll do it?"

The plane shook as a jet roared past them from behind. Jen jumped, Grant swore, and Mark held on to the wheel as the plane bucked in the back draft. Zeke leaned forward, peering out the front window. "Now that was some awesome sauce. Where'd it go?"

"N400204. You are nearing the no-fly zone. Turn back immediately or you will be downed."

Jen clicked the mic. "Shoot us down and Dr. Cartwright won't get the data we brought from Dr. Wilson."

Silence.

"Did you hear me, Fairchild? We have the shit to save the world."

"N400204, stand by."

Jen wriggled her eyebrows. "You've just got to know what makes them tick."

Mark grinned and shook his head. "The shit to save the world, huh?"

Two jets maneuvered into position off each of the Cessna's wings.

"N400204, proceed to my location and land from the southwest. Our fighters will escort you."

Jen handed the mic back to Mark. "See, that's the way it's done."

The jets moved farther to the side, the sun glinting off their canopies.

"I don't get it," Grant said. "What do they think we're gonna do with a little plane like this?"

"They want to make sure we're not zombies," Zeke said, his eyes still on his manga.

Mark banked the plane. "Everyone buckle in. We'll be on the ground in a minute." He picked up the mic. "N400204 to Control. Preparing for landing."

"Roger, N400204. You may proceed. Park at the northeast end of the runway and turn off your engines."

"Roger."

Grant coughed. "Guess there'll be a welcoming committee."

The plane slowed and its nose dipped. The base came into view, its runway lined with hangars and other buildings. A concrete wall encircled the entire base except a couple hundred yards of the southwest corner.

"Holy shit," Jen said. "I've never heard of an Air Force base with a wall before."

"That's because there's never been one," Mark said. "They got that damn thing up in record time."

Grant leaned forward. "That wall's got to be at least twenty feet tall." He pointed. "And look. Guard towers."

"And that open part's got all that construction equipment," Jen said. "Looks like they plan to finish it, but I don't see anyone there."

Zeke sat up and yawned. "Maybe they're all at breakfast."

The Cessna descended toward the runway. A fire truck

with its lights flashing was parked at the northeast end of the runway. Several Humvees sped toward the same spot.

The plane settled on the tarmac and Mark hit the brakes, guiding the aircraft to stop near the fire truck. He turned off the engine. "Leave the weapons. We don't need them on base, and I don't want to give anyone an excuse to get nervous and shoot."

Zeke gently put his scabbard on the seat. "I don't like leaving Betty unsecured."

"Betty?" Jen asked. "You've named your sword?"

"Of course," Zeke said. "All great men have named their swords. Haven't you heard of Stormbringer, Oathkeeper, and Excalibur?"

"And now Betty," Jen said. "Sure rolls off the tongue."

Mark opened the door. "Let's get out there before they come in and get us."

They exited the plane. Mark put his hands up and the others followed suit.

Two Humvees flanked the fire truck. Gunners with machine guns aimed their weapons at them from atop the Humvees, the vehicles' throaty engines idling.

Jen waved at them. "Hey. You want to come out and play?"

The fire engine rumbled off, revealing two squads lined up in hazmat suits and carrying M4s. One soldier stood to the side, pistol holstered on his hip.

Jen cupped her hands to the sides of her mouth and yelled over the roar of the receding fire truck, which had black smoke belching from its exhaust. "Are those rifles in your hands or are you just happy to see us?"

The pistol soldier barked an unintelligible order, and seventeen rifles snapped to and pointed at the newcomers.

2

Mark raised his hands in the air, a gesture copied by Jen and the others.

The soldier with the pistol stepped forward. "I'm Sergeant Howell. Are you armed?"

"No," Mark said. "We left our weapons on board the plane."

Howell nodded. "Is the data for Dr. Cartwright on the plane, too?"

Jen stepped forward, and half the rifles pointed at her. She froze. "I have it. In my pants pocket."

"Your name?" Howell asked.

"Jen. Jen Reed."

"Jen Reed," Howell said. "Slowly remove the items from your pocket."

She eased her right hand into the pocket, grasped the thumb drive and vial, and removed her hand. She held her hand out and opened it. Howell strode to her side, his hazmat suit crinkling with each step. He pointed his pistol at her chest, then nodded at the vial. "What's that?"

"The original spores carrying the virus."

Howell stepped back, holstered his pistol, and removed a plastic bag from a pouch in his suit. He took the thumb drive and vial and placed them in the bag before sealing it.

He turned and Jen said, "Wait."

Howell paused, then continued back to his position beside his men. "What is it, Jen Reed?"

"Can I see Dr. Cartwright?"

"She's not here. She's in CDC Headquarters in Atlanta. We'll transfer the digital data and send the vial on a military transport."

Jen frowned. She needed to talk to Cartwright. "Then I guess we'll just be moving on. You wouldn't be able to spare some fuel, would you?"

"I'm afraid you won't be going anywhere just yet," Howell said. "You'll be put in quarantine for twenty-four hours, just to be safe."

"Why?" Grant said. "If you're worried about us turning, you'd be better off letting us go."

Howell put a hand out, palm down, and lowered it. The soldiers shouldered their weapons. He gestured to Mark. "You can all put your hands down."

Zeke made an exaggerated showing of wringing his arms out. "My arms were getting sore."

"You can't leave yet," Howell said. "Dr. Cartwright may have some questions for you once she gets the data. Besides, it's Colonel Butler's orders."

"Butler?" Jen said. "You mean the same dickhead that abandoned us in Anchorage and flew off with his tail between his legs?"

A few of the soldiers looked at each other and scuffled their feet. Howell remained still. "Colonel Butler is the commander of this installation and he answers directly to

Dr. Cartwright. Orders are you all stay in quarantine for twenty-four hours."

He pointed to a one-story, nondescript building twenty yards behind him. "That's the quarantine facility. You'll have showers, beds, and food." When no one moved, he said, "I assure you it's only for a day."

Jen frowned. "Not giving us much of a choice." She shuffled toward the building, her friends following.

The front door opened into a long hallway down the side of the building. On the right was a door and a long window. Howell opened the door. "In here, please."

Five sets of bunk beds lined the walls, while a long table and chairs sat in the middle of the room. A door marked "Bathroom/Showers" stood on the back wall. An acrid odor stung Jen's nostrils, causing her to sneeze. The place smelled like it had just been scrubbed down with every cleaning chemical known to man.

"Cozy," Jen said. "I'd like to take a shower and not have to get back into these nasty clothes."

"We'll find you some fresh clothes," Howell said.

Zeke raised his hand. "I have extra clothes on the plane."

Howell appraised him for a moment, then nodded and closed the door. The lock tumblers clinked.

Howell appeared at the window, and his voice came from the speaker above it. "I'll inform Colonel Butler that you're here."

Jen waited until he left to speak. "I don't like living in a damn fishbowl."

Grant went into the bathroom and came out a minute later. "Facilities look good."

Mark stretched out on a bottom bunk. "Might as well get some rest. We'll be back in the air in twenty-four hours."

Zeke stood in front of a case of MREs. He opened it,

lifted one out, and examined the package. "Veggie omelet. Wonder how this tastes?"

Grant made a retching sound. "I got one of those on deployment. I'd rather eat sand. There's a reason everyone called it a 'Vomelet.'"

"I could use something to eat, too," Jen said. She picked out an MRE and plopped onto a bed. "I hope they get those clothes here soon. I can't stand my own smell."

Grant rummaged through the MREs. "It's all shit."

Mark had lain back on the bed with his hands behind his head. "Pretty much the definition of MREs."

Zeke opened his package and shoveled food into his mouth like there was no tomorrow. Grant watched him, disgust and disbelief alternating on his face.

A click came over the speaker. Howell stood to one side of the window in BDUs and with his hazmat suit removed. Beside him stood a barrel-chested man with close-cropped red hair that thinned in the front. He had a neutral look on his face and eagles on his collar. *Butler.*

"I trust you're comfortable," he said.

Jen scowled. "Trust isn't a word you should be using with us."

Mark gave her an imperceptible headshake.

Butler acted as if he hadn't heard her. "You're the scientist." He pointed at Grant. "And the guardsman."

Grant stood at attention. "Yes, sir."

Kiss ass.

"Once you pass quarantine, you'll join one of my units."

"Sir?"

"The president has nationalized the guard and reserves."

Grant's face dropped. *Poor guy will never get back to Kodiak now.*

Butler pointed at Mark, whose jaw tightened. "Who are you?"

"Mark Colton. I was security for Doc."

Butler's eyebrows rose. "Bang-up job you did."

Mark's face grew dark. *I wouldn't want to be Butler if Mark gets pissed at him.*

Butler put his hands on his hips. "We have the scientist of the group, the guardsman, and the security man." He nodded at Zeke, who still sat at the table stuffing his face and getting half of it on his ninja costume. "Who the hell is he?"

Jen shrugged. "He's our ninja."

"Colonel," Mark said, "we delivered the data to you for Dr. Cartwright. We'd like to move on. How about we just get our plane fueled and fly out of here?"

Jen tilted her head to the side. Mark's jaw muscles were still tight and his was voice clipped.

The door's deadbolt clunked and it opened. Two soldiers stood there, one holding a gun aimed at Jen and the others, the other walking in with a pile of clothes. He dropped them on the floor. The two soldiers backed out and closed the door.

Howell pointed to the clothes pile. "BDUs in various sizes. One is bound to fit each of you."

Zeke stood. "What about my—"

"We got one of your extra costumes from the plane," Howell said. "It's at the bottom of the pile."

Zeke pulled his shirt over his head, revealing a thin, but muscled body covered in tattoos. "Awesome. I'm ready for a change."

Jen put a hand to her eyes. "Don't ever do that again, Nerd Boy. And go take a shower first. You smell like a fresh turd in the middle of summer."

There was a click. Butler spoke to Howell, but it didn't come over the speaker. Howell saluted and strode off.

Another click and Butler said, "If there's nothing else, then I have plenty of other issues to tend to."

He turned.

"Wait," Mark said.

Butler turned back, his eyebrows raised.

"What about the plane and the fuel? We'd be out of your hair in no time."

The colonel leaned forward and the speaker clicked. "The plane is ours. Specialist Grant there is ours. The rest of you will leave once your quarantine is up, but you'll leave on foot."

3

J en walked out of the bathroom with her hair wet and her new BDUs snug, but comfortable.

The door clicked, then opened. Sergeant Howell stood there.

"Been a change of plans," he said. "Cartwright wants to speak to you."

Finally get to speak to someone with some sense.

Howell had his pistol holstered. No other soldiers were in sight.

"I'm up for it." Jen nodded at her friends. "But they come with me."

Howell held the door open. "Absolutely."

He led them down a plain-looking hallway, their footsteps on the tiles loud and echoing. Outside the building, Jen took a deep breath of the breezy air. She'd been locked up for less than a day and it felt like a month.

Howell led them to an awaiting Humvee and paused as a helicopter rose from a nearby helipad. When its sound receded, Howell said, "You'll find an M4 and M9 Beretta with holster and ammo inside the Humvee for each of you. No one goes unarmed, even on base."

"What about my katana?" Zeke asked.

"Your melee weapons are in there, too."

"Solid." Zeke jumped in and grabbed his katana, cradling it like a lover. Jen shoved her axe into her belt and strapped on the 9mm.

Howell put the Humvee into gear and took off, navigating past troop formations and heavy vehicle traffic. A helicopter passed overhead as the Humvee stopped in front a long one-story building with a sign that said "Headquarters" on it.

Howell led them inside at a clipped pace. He stopped at a natural wood door and rapped his knuckles on it.

"Enter."

Howell opened the door and gestured for the others to go in.

Jen entered the room. A long conference table lay in the middle, chairs around it. Blackout curtains kept the room dim, with overhead LEDs providing light. Butler sat at the head of the table and the other seats were empty.

A sixty-inch video monitor hung on the wall across from the door. Dr. Cartwright's curt face was displayed on it.

"Come in and have a seat," she said. "Quickly now, I have a lot to do."

Jen sat and leaned forward on her elbows while the others took seats around her. Jen glanced at Butler. He sat ramrod straight, his eyes focusing on some unknown point on the wall.

Jen said, "Dr. Cartwright—"

"First, let me thank you for delivering the vial and data," Cartwright said. "We've received the data digitally and are processing it. The vial should arrive later today by military transport."

She paused, staring at Jen.

Jen cleared her throat. "You're welcome."

Cartwright gave a short nod. "I would like to know about Dr. Wilson." The muscles in her face loosened and she blinked several times.

Is she going to cry?

"I'd like—no, I need to know about his final minutes."

Jen's pulse picked up. She'd shoved Doc's death into the back of her mind with all the other bad crap, and now she had to pull it out and relive it.

I got him killed.

She took a deep breath. "He wondered what turning would be like."

"And?"

Jen lowered her voice. "It was painful."

Mark's head lowered. Cartwright visibly swallowed, but her expression remained the same. Her glasses had slid to the tip of her nose, and she tilted her head forward and peered over them at Jen. "What else...what else did he say?"

"He gave me the thumb drive and vial and asked me to get it here. To get it to you."

Cartwright nodded. "Even then, his last thoughts were on helping others."

She took her glasses off and rubbed her eyes before putting them back on. "And there was nothing else?"

Jen squared her shoulders. That was her opening. "He said to tell you he recommends I work with you. He'd planned on making me his assistant, and he thought I should work for you once he was gone."

Butler scoffed.

"Did he?" Cartwright asked.

Jen narrowed her eyes. "Yes."

"Colonel Butler, can you and your sergeant give us a moment, please?" Cartwright said.

Butler shook his head like he hadn't heard correctly. "You want me to leave?"

"Yes, Colonel. Please."

Butler stood, tight-lipped, and stalked out the door.

Cartwright picked a paper up from her desk. "I printed out all of Doc's notes and reports, and this letter jumped out at me. It's addressed to me. Besides other, more personal things, he mentions just what you said. That you should work for me."

Jen looked at Mark, who raised an eyebrow, then back at Cartwright. "OK. So is there a problem?"

"How do I know you didn't add that to his letter after he died?"

Jen shot out of her seat. "What? Why would I do that?"

Cartwright looked over her glasses at Jen. Jen waited for her to say something, but she just stared. Jen sat down.

"If you worked for me," Cartwright said, "you'd have resources available to you like food, transportation, and shelter. That's a lot more than most survivors."

"When would I have changed it? Doc gave it to me right before he died. We were out in the city and on the run."

Cartwright's eyes never left Jen's. "How do I know that? He could've given it to you before you left the lab. Plenty of computers there to hop on. Or maybe you found one in the city."

Jen laughed. "Sure. In a totaled city with zombies and asshole humans trying to kill us at every turn, we stopped somewhere that miraculously had power, just so I could see what was on a thumb drive."

Mark interrupted. "What Jen says is true. I was there when Doc died."

"Me, too," Grant said.

Cartwright's unflinching gaze swept over each of them in turn and landed on Zeke, who was examining the ninja hood in his hands. "What about the man in black?"

"Nope. I was busy with those assholes Jen mentioned."

"I see." Cartwright adjusted her glasses and sighed. "Until I have more proof than that, I'm afraid I can't honor the request. I therefore must release you to Colonel Butler."

"Wait," Jen said.

Cartwright's hand had moved to the bottom of the screen. She pulled it back. "Yes?"

"Something Doc said. It's on the tip of my tongue."

"Please don't waste my time, Miss Reed."

"It's not Miss Reed. It's Jen." She had to remember. What was it Doc said? *Think. Bug. Something about a bug.*

"I'll eat a bug if it isn't true," she blurted out.

Cartwright leaned closer to the camera, her mouth hanging slightly open. "What did you say?"

"Doc told me to tell you that he'd eat a bug if it isn't true."

A smile spread across Cartwright's face, and her eyes glistened. "That son of a bitch."

Cartwright sat back. "I believe you, Jen. There's never been a person on this earth I've trusted more than John Wilson."

Cartwright's smile faded. "Back to business. Jen, I'd like to offer you that assistant position. Will you take it?"

Jen glanced at Mark, who grinned and shook his head like he couldn't believe it. Grant sat, nodding at her. Zeke gazed at a wall.

Jen straightened in her chair. "Yes, Dr. Cartwright. I do accept."

"Good," Cartwright said. "Young man?"

Zeke looked around. "Me?"

"Yes. Please ask the colonel and sergeant to step back in."

Zeke walked to the door, opened it, and said, "She wants you back."

Colonel Butler strode in and took a position by the door. Sergeant Howell stood a few feet to his left, his hands clasped behind his back.

"Colonel."

"Yes, Doctor."

"Jen answers only to me, and will receive all cooperation and support needed for her to perform her mission."

To his credit, Butler didn't strangle on the words, but he looked like he'd just swallowed a shit sandwich. "Yes, Doctor."

Jen glanced at Mark. What about him? "My first request is to have Mark, Grant, and Zeke assist me."

Cartwright sighed. "I can authorize the big guy and the skinny ninja. But the president activated the National Guard, and your friend there is under Colonel Butler's command."

Grant looked at Jen with a hangdog expression. She'd figure a way to spring him.

"When do we get out of here?" Mark asked.

Cartwright steepled her fingers. "A week. I need you to go outside the base and record observations of zombie behavior. Dr. Wilson's notes mention a possible mutation and behavior changes. We need current data."

Butler grunted. "They're just a bunch of dumb meat bags."

Mark glared at Butler. *Yeah, Mark. I'm still pissed he left us in Anchorage, too.*

"Why stay here and study them? Hasn't the virus made it to Atlanta?" Jen asked.

Cartwright frowned and looked to her side for a moment. Was someone else there with her?

"It has made it to almost every corner of the globe," Cartwright said. "We lost the west coast before we could do anything. But the government initiated protocols to more closely monitor population deaths to neutralize the deceased before they can turn."

Mark squinted his eyes. "Protocols?"

Cartwright ignored him. "So there are very few zombies here to study, while Fairchild is at the front lines." She locked eyes with Jen. "That is why I need you there for now."

"And then we go to Atlanta," Jen stated. "Makes sense. I'll get the data you need."

"Good," Cartwright said. She reached for the screen and paused. "Doc didn't give false praise. The way he described you tells me we'll make great strides together. I'll be in touch."

The screen went blank. Butler crossed his arms. "I expect you'll complete your mission and get the hell off my base. We're in a war zone, and I don't need civilians running around and getting in the way."

Mark's hands clenched, his knuckles turning white. "You didn't do too well in Afghanistan with your military troops, either."

Butler glared at him. "Sergeant," he barked. "Show them to their rooms and the dining hall." He pointed at Grant. "Except the specialist. Assign him to a recon unit. He's been in the middle of the shit already. Might as well take advantage of his experience."

An alarm blared from speakers on the wall. Jen flinched and covered her ears.

Howell grabbed a phone that had no dial buttons. The alarm stopped, and Howell barked into the mouthpiece, "What direction? How many?"

He slammed the phone into the cradle. "Sir, attack from the southwest. Estimated strength in the thousands."

4

J en piled into the idling Humvee outside the Headquarters building, sitting between Mark and Zeke. Butler sat up front while Howell jumped into the driver's seat. Looking glum, Grant sat in back.

Howell put the vehicle in gear and drove like a bat out of hell, arriving at the unfinished southwest wall in minutes.

Twenty yards past where they parked, the wall ended. Construction equipment sat quiet as soldiers took up firing positions back from the perimeter.

Butler strode toward a platform against the wall on a hydraulic lift. "Stay with me," he barked.

When the last of them boarded, Howell hit a button on a control box and the platform rose in the air. Other platforms with armed men were already in the air, just above the wall.

Howell handed Butler a radio and he keyed the mic. "Where's the damn Apache? And I haven't seen that C-130 take off yet."

Static burst from the radio, then a voice said, "Hotel Four on the way, sir. Fully loaded. C-130 is taxiing for takeoff."

They reached the top of the wall and Jen's heart skipped. Zombies raced toward the base, as far as she could see.

The helicopter swooped behind their platform and hovered, facing the perimeter.

Jen spoke into Mark's ear. "Is that helicopter the Apache he asked for?"

Mark nodded. "It's a two-seater that's armed for bear. I saw a Blackhawk parked on the tarmac on the way over here. They carry a punch, too, but are also good for transport."

Howell yelled over the thumping of the rotor blades. "One of our recon planes spotted them heading this way. Some will hit the wall and we'll wipe them up, but others will stumble into the gap in the wall."

The lead wave of zombies crashed against the wall to Jen's right, and the soldiers stationed there opened fire.

Zombies went down, but more filled their spots faster than the soldiers could keep up.

Machine gun bursts from her left had Jen ducking and looking that way. A sea of zombies had breached the open perimeter and the helicopter had opened fire, along with a couple hundred soldiers and several Humvee-mounted .50 cal machine guns.

They were barely keeping up. What the hell would happen when they had to reload?

Colonel Butler pointed to the sky. "There it is."

A C-130 gunship appeared and flew high over the distant trees. It banked and spit fire from its side. Hundreds of zombies fell.

"I've gotta get me one of those," Mark said.

Grant watched the plane bank and come around for another run. "You're not kidding."

Jen grinned. "What do you think, Zeke?"

She glanced behind her, then turned. Zeke wasn't on the platform. "Shit."

"What?" Howell asked.

"Zeke is doing his ninja shit again," she said.

Mark pointed down to the line of soldiers holding back the horde. Zeke stood behind them, his hood on and his katana ready. When the soldiers in front of him reloaded, Zeke jumped out and sliced through the lead zombies, felling several and keeping the others back. When the next shots fired, he ducked behind the line.

They stopped to reload again, and like a dancer, Zeke sprung forward, his katana singing through the air and into undead flesh. Sunlight glinted off the blade as he stepped forward, sliced, spun, and beheaded another zombie. Then he ducked and stepped back to take out another.

Entranced, Jen could only watch. *That little shit really is a ninja.*

The C-130 burped another storm of death, and hundreds more zombies bit the big one.

Butler put his hands on his hips. "Damn good job." He keyed the radio mic. "Order ground units forward on mop-up. Have Hotel One fly cover and the gunship return home."

"Yes, sir," came from the radio.

"And transition to cleanup operations as soon as the all clear is reported."

"Yes, Colonel."

The Humvees and ground troops pushed past the perimeter. The occasional gunshot barked, but it seemed as if the horde had been destroyed.

More troops moved forward with flamethrower tanks on their backs.

Mark pointed at them. "Clean up?"

Howell nodded. "Too many to bury. Too many to stack

and burn. Who knows what other diseases they're carrying?"

"Sergeant, take us down and back to Headquarters," Butler said.

Howell pushed a button and the platform lowered to the ground. Zeke stood off to the side, talking with a soldier. He'd cleaned off his katana blade, but his costume was splattered with blood and innards.

Jen waved to him as she walked to the Humvee. "Come on, Zeke. We're heading back."

Zeke was the last to get in. He pulled his hood off and had the biggest shit-eating grin Jen had seen on his face.

"That was a blast," he said.

"You did a hell of a job," Grant said.

Zeke shrugged. "That was only the first level. Can't wait to move up to the second level."

"What does that even mean?" Grant asked.

Jen grinned. "It's a nerd thing."

Zeke winked. "Damn straight."

Howell parked at the Headquarters building and Butler stepped out. "Show them to their rooms and the chow hall, then get Specialist Grant to his new unit. I want them done with their mission and out of my hair." He strode into the building.

Howell guided them inside and down a long hallway to a T intersection. A sign in front of them pointed left to the dining facility.

"Dining facility?" Jen said. "Sounds fancy."

Mark shrugged. "It's a chow hall with a fancy name."

Howell pointed down the hallway to the right. "Rooms are down here."

He led them past two more hallways, and they came to lobby with a soldier behind a desk.

"Smitty," Howell said. "You have the keys for those rooms?"

The soldier reached under the counter and handed Howell three sets of keys. "Fresh linen, cleaned, and aired out."

"Thanks." Howell handed the keys out. "I suggest the first thing you do is go get some chow. You never know when the shit'll hit the fan around here and you'll go without until it's over."

"Specialist Grant, you're with me." Howell strode away, Grant by his side.

Zeke sniffed. "I'm starving."

Jen looked at Mark and raised her eyebrows. "I could eat," he said.

Ten minutes later, they sat in the empty chow hall, a tray of food in front of each of them.

Jen cut her roast beef and gave Mark a sidelong glance. "What's with you and Butler? I mean, other than him leaving us high and dry in Anchorage, the asshole."

Mark paused mid-chew, then swallowed. He took a sip of coffee. "Was it that obvious?"

"It was obvious you don't like him." Zeke slurped soup off his spoon.

Jen shrugged. "You said something about Afghanistan."

Mark put his coffee cup down and wiped his mouth with a napkin. He looked around and dropped his voice. "I'll tell you what I know. But you have to keep it to yourself."

Jen nodded. Mark turned to Zeke. He'd given up on the spoon and had picked up the bowl and slurped even louder from there.

"How about you?" Mark asked.

Zeke put the bowl down and wiped his mouth with his sleeve. "I can keep a secret."

"I didn't make the connection when we heard his name back in Anchorage," Mark said. "But the minute I saw that flat-top carrot head, I had no doubt it was him."

"What about him?" Jen asked.

Mark leaned on the table and clasped his hands together. "I never served directly with him, but did serve with some that did. Butler had a reputation of risking his men's lives for a mission."

"Isn't that what all commanders do?" Jen asked. "Isn't it a risk any time they go out?"

Mark scowled. "Not like this guy. He'd send them out when he could've waited for more troops and kept the death count down. No, all he cared about was the objective."

"Kinda like the Joker," Zeke said.

Mark ignored him and continued. "It wasn't just the grunts. He had a major who pushed back and argued with him. The major stuck up for his men and Butler didn't like it.

"So they're out on a mission, and when it came time for extraction, the major and three of his men stayed in the rear to cover everyone else."

Mark paused and took a drink. "The Taliban attacked, but the colonel and his men made it to the helicopters. All he had to do was have his men lay down cover fire while the major and his men beat feet to join them. Instead he ordered the helicopters to leave."

Jen clenched her teeth. The same damn thing he'd done to them in Anchorage. "What happened to the major?"

Mark faced her, his upper lip curled back as he spat out the words. "Remember those four soldiers that were kept hostage by the Taliban and were beheaded one at a time over six months?"

Jen's stomach soured. "No telling what that asshole would do to us."

Zeke finished his soup and put the bowl down. He let out an exaggerated sigh. "Lucky for us we'll be gone in a week." His face clouded. "But not Grant."

"Don't you worry about that," Jen said. "I've got leverage with Cartwright and I'm going to use it. I'll get Grant out of here."

Howell strode into the chow hall. "I'm glad you took my advice."

Jen caught Mark's eyes. They'd have to be more careful where they talked freely. Howell could've walked in during their conversation.

Mark gestured to an empty chair pulled up to the table. "Join us, Sergeant?"

Howell put his hands on his hips. "Not this time. You're going to join me and Colonel Butler."

"What for?" Jen asked.

"Colonel's taking you on a mission. We're to meet him at the helipad in ten minutes."

"We get to ride in a chopper?" Zeke asked.

Jen winced. *Yeah, we'll ride out in it, but will we come back in it?*

5

H owell stopped at a metal door just inside the lobby. He banged his fist on it and yelled, "Howell here. Need ammo loads now."

A small door opened and closed, then the metal door swung open. A shirtless soldier stepped to the side and let them in. "Whatcha lookin' for, Sarge?"

Howell positioned himself at the center of the room and Jen stopped next to him. Weapons lined every wall. Racks of M4 Carbines against one wall, with pistols and machine guns along another.

"Need M4 and 9mm loads for each of these folks," Howell said. "Going shopping in the city."

Jen walked over to the machine guns. "These look pretty nice."

"M60s," Howell said. "Sorry, but you're not authorized."

The armorer stacked the ammo on a desk. "Here ya go."

Zeke stood across the room admiring the flamethrowers. He glanced back and jerked a thumb at the rack in front of him. "Mind if I take one of these instead?"

The armorer looked at Howell.

"Fuck, no," Howell said. "You all get standard load out. Get your ass over here and grab your rounds."

Zeke shrugged. "Can't blame me for trying." He took a sling of 5.56 ammo for his rifle.

"You know how to handle that weapon?" the armorer asked.

"I have a master badge on my M4 Carbine. I love this gun."

"Master badge?" The armorer squinted. "Never heard of that before. Where'd you get it?"

"FPS," Zeke said.

"FPS?"

Zeke slung the rifle over his shoulder. "First Person Shooter."

Mark took pistol ammo from the armorer. "You don't want to know."

"Load it all up," Howell said.

Jen followed Howell outside. It had cooled and dark clouds had rolled in, covering the base in a dusk-like shadow.

Howell climbed into the driver's seat of an extended cab pickup. Jen and the others joined him.

As much as it was an understatement, Zeke looked awkward—a skinny kid with a rifle, pistol, and sword. "How are you going to manage all of those weapons?" she asked.

Zeke winked at her and lowered his voice. "Once we get into any real action, I'll hide the rifle and take out Betty." He patted the scabbard.

Jen rubbed her face. "For your sake, I hope this zombie apocalypse doesn't end too soon. I don't know if there's room for you in the place called normal."

Howell put the truck in gear and took off.

THE MUFFLED *WHUMP whump* of helicopter blades signaled they'd arrived at the helipad. The truck stopped ten yards from the helicopter and they all got out.

"Follow me," Howell yelled. He hurried to the helicopter, bending over as he got closer. Jen mimicked his movements.

"This is a Blackhawk," Mark said to Jen.

The colonel sat in the front seat with the pilot, his headset on. Howell seated each of them and made sure their belts were secure, then gave the pilot a thumbs-up.

The helicopter lifted a few feet off the ground, then tilted and flew forward while it gained altitude.

Butler turned and yelled over the helicopter's racket to Jen. "Dr. Cartwright wants you to observe. We've got a roundup in progress and I thought it'd give you a chance to see what we've been doing. At the same time you can observe the zombies."

They flew over the wall and across countryside to the highway. Nothing moved below, the cars and trucks parked at weird angles and looking like toys.

"What's a roundup?" Jen yelled back.

"You'll see, Miss Reed. You'll see."

Jen didn't remind him to call her by her first name like she'd done with everyone else.

The helicopter flew over the city. Abandoned cars littered the streets, along with a few shuffling undead, but it was mostly just a graveyard. Butler pointed off in the distance and looked at the pilot. The pilot nodded and the chopper shifted to fly in that direction.

Mark sat quiet, almost trance-like. *He's flown these things plenty of times, so it's no big deal to him.*

They slowed as they came to the larger buildings in the city. The helicopter descended toward the top of the tallest building ahead of them. Jen braced herself for it to hit hard, but it landed so smoothly she almost couldn't feel it.

The pilot flipped some switches on his console and the blades slowed down. "You can remove your restraints at this time."

Howell unlatched his belt, pulled the door open, and stepped onto the rooftop. Jen and the others followed him out.

Butler led them to the edge of the roof and pointed below. Several shorter buildings flanked the one they stood on, lining up to create a U shape, with their building at the bottom of the U.

Jen looked at Mark, but he didn't break his eyes away from the troops assembled on top of the other buildings. Set up with machine guns and other small arms, they faced the inner part of the U.

"This is our roundup," Butler said. "We had a recon unit go out and stir up the meat bags. They're leading them here as we speak."

He pointed to the streets below. "Every side street is blocked off with vehicles, except for that one directly below us. That's where the recon vehicle gets out after luring them here."

"What keeps them from following your men out of there?" Mark asked.

Butler shaded his eyes and scanned the area. "You'll see."

Jen shifted the rifle on her shoulder. "Then it's shooting-fish-in-a-barrel time."

Butler smiled. "Exactly. So you see that we're taking care of business here. Eliminating the threat a few hundred and a few thousand at a time."

"Sir." Howell pointed to the left. A Humvee drove up a two-lane street bordered by an open park on one side and a lake on the other. A horde raced after it. Several zombies strayed, and the Humvee honked its horn, keeping them locked on the vehicle. The deluge of zombies kept coming. There had to be several hundred.

Butler pulled a handheld radio from his belt and brought it to his mouth. "Command One to all units. Targets in sight. Prepare to engage."

The soldiers on the rooftops, who had been lounging and smoking, gathered their weapons and set up.

Zeke had wandered off, exploring. *He gets bored easy.*

The Humvee paused at the opening of the trap, then traveled down the street between the buildings, the hungry horde clamoring behind it. Just before it would've hit her building, the vehicle took a sharp left and zoomed down the open road. A moving van parked on the side of the road roared to life and pulled across the road, blocking it. A soldier hopped out and scurried away.

The horde hit the dead end and stopped. Having no prey in sight, they milled around.

Butler put the radio to his mouth. "Commence firing."

The immediate blast of gunfire made Jen cringe and take a step back. The troops on both sides poured rifle and machine gun fire into the zombies and they fell like flies.

Five minutes later, commanders shouted to cease fire. Not a zombie moved.

"Shit," Jen said, her ears ringing. "There had to be five or six hundred of them."

Butler turned to her. "This is what we do, Miss Reed. We take out the enemy. It's just a matter of time before we have them all."

"But you still have the virus to deal with," Mark said.

"Dr. Cartwright and her team will take care of that."

Butler smirked at Jen. "Did you observe any behavior you need to report back?"

Pompous asshole. "Not much to observe if they're all dead."

"Precisely why you're wasting your time here," Butler said.

Would it be too obvious if I accidentally tripped and knocked him off the roof?

"Jen," Zeke called from behind.

She glanced over her shoulder, then spun. Zeke stood over two headless zombies. "Where the hell did they come from?"

Zeke wiped his katana off on their ragged clothes. "Door on the other side of the roof. It opens facing the other way, so we didn't see it when we got here."

Howell pushed the corpses with his toe. "Good job, soldier."

Zeke pulled his hood off. "I'm a ninja. If I was a soldier, I would've been over there with you guys, not hearing these zombies coming because of all the gunfire."

Mark smiled. "He's got a point."

Butler grunted and stalked to the helicopter. "Back to base. Cleanup crews will take care of the bodies."

Jen peered down to the street. Dozens of soldiers with flamethrowers had already begun.

AFTER LANDING AT THE BASE, Butler drove off in a staff car without a word.

Fine with me.

Howell dropped them off at the HQ building. "You're safe to get some rest for a while, unless there's an attack on the base."

"Are we free to walk around?" Mark asked.

Howell shrugged. "Sure. Everywhere except the restricted areas designated by Colonel Butler."

"Where are those?" Jen asked.

"Here and there," Howell said. "They're clearly marked and have guards posted."

Zeke squinted at Howell. "Why would you have restricted areas here? There's only soldiers on the base and the zombies aren't going to try sneaking in."

Jen chuckled. He sometimes acted odd, but Zeke had it together.

"Even soldiers have varying security clearance levels," Howell said. He climbed into the truck, rolled down the window, and stuck his head out. "Just stay away from those areas. The guards are armed and take their jobs seriously."

He put the truck in gear and drove off.

Jen propped her hands on her hips and raised her eyebrows. "If it's something Colonel Butthead doesn't want us to know about, then it must be worth looking at, if only to piss him off. Who wants to go find some restricted areas with me?"

6

J en stopped on a corner. Several soldiers and an airman passed her, ignored Mark, and stared at Zeke.

Jen nudged Zeke. "I guess that sneaky ninja stuff works better at night."

Zeke sniffed. "I could make myself invisible during the day, too. Just no reason to do it now."

Mark shook his head, smiling.

Jen frowned. A large, square building stood on the corner lot behind them, its sign indicating it was the supply warehouse. Across the street from it lay an identical building, its large doors open. Armed soldiers drove forklifts amid stacked pallets.

The base fire department sat on the third corner, and on the last one was a small medical clinic.

"Haven't seen anything restricted," Jen said. "Were they just screwing with us?"

Mark shaded his eyes and peered down the street. He pointed. "There. See that?"

Several buildings down there was a gap, then barbwiretopped fencing wrapped around a building. "Ah. Where there's a fence, there's something interesting," Jen said.

She strode down the sidewalk, with Mark at her side and Zeke trailing behind. As they got closer, the full building came into view. Square, five stories, and with no windows, it seemed familiar.

"Looks a bit like our facility in Anchorage," Mark said.

Jen nodded. That was it. But the Anchorage building didn't have a fence.

The only visible door faced the sidewalk they walked along. A gate with an armed guard stood between the door and the road.

As they neared, a car stopped and a short man with balding gray hair and glasses hopped out. His cheap-looking suit was a size too big and the jacket fluttered in a gust of wind.

"Wonder who that is," Jen said. "First non-soldier I've seen here." *Didn't Butler rant about not wanting civilians on base?*

The guard opened the gate, nodded at the man, and closed it after he entered.

Jen slowed as she passed. The man put his hand in a box next to the door and a green light came on as the door opened. Before it closed, she caught sight of a long lit hallway with several soldiers standing along it.

"You need to move along," the guard said.

His voice grabbed Jen's attention. She looked at him, then realized she wasn't moving. Mark and Zeke had gone a few yards past the gate and turned around.

"Sorry," she murmured. "Lost in my thoughts."

The guard glared as she caught up with Mark and Zeke. When they were out of earshot, Mark nudged her. "What did you see?"

She shook her head. "A hallway and some guards. No telling what the hell's going on in there."

They turned at the corner, heading back toward the HQ building.

"Who do you think that guy in the suit was?" Zeke asked.

Mark stopped and put out his arms, causing Jen and Zeke to halt.

"Let's not get all tinfoil hat about this." He pointed past them. Jen turned. On the roof of the restricted building stood a tall, heavy antenna.

"Communications," Mark said. "Always restricted."

Jen put her hands on her hips. *Was that all it was?* She felt like an ass.

She pushed past Mark. "I don't know about you guys, but I could use another meal and some sleep."

A WEEK later she turned off the shower and toweled off. *Funny how you miss the little things when you don't have them.*

Her dresser had more military clothing her size, so she put on a fresh set and headed to the chow hall.

The place was almost full, but she spotted Zeke at a corner table with one plate stacked with pancakes and another brimming with eggs, bacon, and home fries. The smell of the bacon made her mouth water.

She grabbed some scrambled eggs and bacon and joined Zeke. He had just drowned his pancakes in half a bottle of fake maple syrup. "What's our plan today?" he asked.

Jen swallowed a mouthful of eggs and picked up a piece of bacon. "I figure I better check in with Cartwright. But after that we need to get out in the field. I'll talk to Howell about getting us a vehicle."

Mark strode into the chow hall looking more relaxed than she'd seen him before.

He made a beeline straight to them and sat down. Leaning forward, he lowered his voice, barely audible over the mixture of conversations and clinking silverware. "Found out more about that restricted area."

Jen swallowed what she had in her mouth, then downed her juice. She glanced at a nearby table, then whispered, "What do you have?"

"I got up early this morning," Mark said, "and went for my run. When I was done, I went to the gym and lifted some weights. There was a guy next to me and we spotted for each other. We started talking, and I just happened to mention the restricted area."

He scooted his chair up a bit and looked around before continuing. "Guy said his barracks roommate was picked for duty at the restricted area. The troops call it Area 51. His roommate moved over to the special barracks for people who work in Area 51. He didn't see the guy for a month."

Mark licked his lips. "When he ran into his buddy again, all he could get out of him was a 'Hey, how are ya doing?' The guy kept his mouth shut and walked away."

Zeke stabbed a sausage patty and held it up, examining it. "Definitely sounds like something strange is going on there."

"It does," Jen said. "And everyone here knows it. Why else call it Area 51?"

Mark shrugged. "Could mean nothing. There's no place on Earth where rumors fly more freely than a military base."

"I'd ask Cartwright about it," Jen said, "but I need to feel her out a little bit more. I'm not sure yet what I can trust her with." She pushed her plate away. "In the meantime, we need to get into the city and see what our zombie friends have been up to."

Zeke pointed his fork at two greasy pieces of bacon on Jen's plate. "You going to eat those?"

Jen shook her head. He stabbed the bacon and shoved it into his mouth. *Where the hell does this skinny kid put all that food?*

"How do we get to the city?" Mark asked.

Jen put a finger in the air. "For that, we need to see the good Sergeant Howell. Rather than getting a vehicle, I think it's safer if we can hitch a ride on the helicopter. Ready?"

Mark stood. Zeke let a quiet belch out and pushed his chair back from the table.

Jen led them out of the chow hall and to the HQ building's lobby, where a disinterested looking guard sat at a desk.

"Where can we find Sergeant Howell?" she asked.

The guard looked them over, then jacked a thumb over his shoulder at a hallway. "Fourth door on your right. Word to the wise: if his door isn't open, make sure you knock."

Jen strode past him and into the hallway. The fourth door stood open, and Howell sat at a desk studying a sheaf of papers.

"Sergeant Howell?" she said.

He looked up and laid the papers down. "Miss Reed and company. What can I do for you?"

"It's Jen," she said. "Do you have any roundups scheduled for today?"

He leaned back in his chair and pointed to a whiteboard. "Schedule's there. Got one in about two hours, and another midafternoon. Why? You didn't get enough of them yesterday?"

Jen raised an eyebrow. "As entertaining as it is to see

hundreds of dead people torn apart, we do have to move on to other things. I'd like to get a ride into the city on the helicopter."

Howell rubbed his chin. "Sure. Do you know where you want to go?"

"Not where your troops will be," Mark said.

Howell stood and stepped to a map of the city next to the whiteboard. "This morning we'll be hitting the northeast section of the city. This afternoon it'll be the western section."

Jen looked at the western section on the map. "What do you think, Mark? We take the west this morning, before they go in and clean it out?"

Mark frowned and inspected the map. He pointed to the northeast. "If the hordes are coming from Seattle and Portland, they'll hit the west first, so I think that's a good call."

Howell folded his arms. "You'll be out there all alone. We'll have no troops in that area until this afternoon, so you'll be stuck in the middle of a ton of zombies and have no immediate backup."

Jen smiled. "Just what I wanted to hear."

7

Crouching, Jen crept to the north end of the rooftop. The thumping of helicopter rotor blades faded in the distance.

A facade on the front of the building rose three feet above the roof's edge and helped her keep a low profile from the thirty or so zombies wandering aimlessly on the railroad tracks twenty yards ahead.

Mark and Zeke took positions on either side of her. "Looks like they didn't take notice of the Blackhawk," Mark said. "How can that be? Damn thing should be drawing every walking corpse within a couple of miles."

Jen shook her head. The undead were still changing. Evolving. "It's like there's something new with them every day."

Zeke tapped her on the shoulder. "I'll check for rooftop entries."

"Good idea," she said. "No surprises. Why don't you also walk the perimeter of the roof and see what we have on all sides? With the way they're acting, we may need all the notice we can get if they attack."

Zeke nodded and stalked off. Muted gunfire came from the northeast. "Guess the roundup has started," Mark said.

Jen grunted. Hopefully, the noise from the roundup would draw any huge hordes away.

She looked down the tracks to the left. A group of nine zombies lumbered in their direction, with one in the lead and the others spread out behind it.

She tapped Mark on the shoulder and nodded toward the incoming zombies. "They're still using formations."

He nodded. "Like geese. Do you notice something else?"

"No," Jen said. "What's that?"

"Listen."

Jen lowered her chin and concentrated on sounds. Other than the distant gunfire and her own breathing, it was pretty quiet. "Not much to hear."

"Exactly," Mark said. "We're close enough to those zombies straight ahead to hear their growling, but there's nothing."

Shit. She listened for any sound from them, but there was still nothing. "That sucks. When they stopped screeching, that took away our main warning system. Even then, we could hear their growling if they were close enough."

Mark wiped a hand down his face. "Now they'll be ninjas, like Zeke."

Zeke slid next to Mark. "There's no ninja like me."

"What'd you find, Grasshopper?" Jen asked.

"Pretty light for zombies. Anywhere from two on one side to five on another." He pointed to the door on the roof. "One point of entry, unless they start scaling walls or flying helicopters."

"Don't laugh," Jen said. "The way they're going, that might be coming."

Mark scoffed. "That's a bit much. I can see them evolving

some instinctual practices, but real thinking? Their brains died."

Jen watched the zombie group in the V formation getting closer. "Who knows what that virus does to the brain?"

Mark's eyebrows rose, but he said nothing.

Zeke pointed to the zombies in formation. "The guy leading them has no visible wounds. Kind of looks like my grandpa at his funeral."

Jen studied the leader, an older man in a dirtied suit. *Looks like he wasn't bitten. Need to remember that for Cartwright.*

Zeke shifted the rifle strapped to his back. "Is this all we're gonna do? Camp up here? Pretty boring, if you ask me."

The kid was right. So far all they'd seen was passive behavior. The information was good, but they'd need to see more of the aggressive, predatory behavior to see if and how it had changed.

"Zeke," she said, "let's stir some shit up, but quietly." She jumped to her feet and waved. Zeke stood next to her, jumping up and down, holding back laughter.

The milling zombies turned as one and streaked straight for them. They hit the rail on the side of the bridge, flipped over, and landed on the street below. A few lay still, but the rest pulled themselves up and hobbled out of sight.

The other group stopped, its leader staring at the rail the first bunch fell over.

Holy shit! Is it thinking?

It turned its head toward Jen, regarding her with yellow eyes. *Damn. He's giving me the creeps.* It sprinted back the way it had come, the others in the group staying in formation.

Jen's mouth hung open and she turned to Mark. "Did you see that? Freaking thing gave me goosebumps."

He swallowed. "Yeah. It's like it learned not to do what the others had."

"Now we've got smart zombie leaders?" Jen said. "What the hell's next?"

Something ran into the inside of the rooftop door. Zeke drew his katana.

Jen and Mark walked toward him. "That's a pretty heavy looking door," Mark said. "One zombie isn't coming through there."

The pounding became more rapid and intense. "That's not just one," Zeke said. "The numbers are going up."

Jen looked around the roof. "Having one entry point is great because you only have to defend one point, but it sucks when you need more escape routes."

"Zeke," Mark said. "Are there other buildings nearby? Anywhere we can escape to?"

The door shuddered from another attack. Zeke pointed to the south side. "One there, but the roof's got a ton of air vents and shit on it, so it would be hard to land there without hitting something." He jerked a thumb to the east. "That one has only one or two. That'd be the best bet."

The doorframe let out a loud crack.

"East side it is." Jen sprinted to that section of the roof. She and Mark peered down as Zeke arrived. The other rooftop was at least a floor lower than the one they stood on. It had no lip on the edge and just a few pipes and vents sticking up.

"Damn," Jen said. "That's a freaking mile across."

Another crack came from the doorframe, and a corner of it pushed out.

Mark took her by her shoulders. "We can jump it." He

looked at Zeke, then back at Jen. "Just remember, go into a roll when you hit the roof. It'll dissipate the energy."

"That's true," Zeke said. "It's a sacred ninja technique."

Jen squinted at him. "You do make me wonder sometimes."

Mark handed Jen his rifle and ran back to the center of the roof. "I'll go first. Show you how to do it. Toss the rifles to me, then make your jumps. Just don't hesitate to come. One at a time."

He sprinted toward the roof's edge, pushed off with a foot and sailed through the air. He landed on a shoulder and rolled a couple of times. He jumped up and ran back to the edge. "Toss the rifles."

Jen heaved his M4 across the alley. He caught it and laid it down. She did the same with hers, then Zeke threw his. Mark took the rifles to the middle of the roof and waved at them. "Come on."

Jen and Zeke ran back to the center where Mark had started. "You go first," Jen said.

"Oh, no," Zeke said. "I know what I'm doing. I can make it easy, no worries. But someone needs to stay on this side when you jump, in case something happens and you need help."

Jen took a deep breath. "Yeah. OK."

Mark yelled, "What are you waiting for?"

Jen crouched in a runner's stance. *You've got it. You've done long jumps before; it's no different. Except the six-story death drop.*

The door burst open and zombies poured onto the roof.

"We both go," Jen yelled. "Now."

A zombie cop streaked for them. Zeke took off and Jen followed. Her pulse pounded in her ears and all she heard above it was her ragged breath and thumping footsteps close behind her.

Zeke made the edge and leapt, his arms windmilling as he soared through the air. He dropped out of sight. *Did he make it?*

The footsteps were almost on her. *Shit shit shit shit shit.*

Five feet from the edge, the other roof came into view. A hand grazed her back. She concentrated on the roof's edge. Somewhere a gunshot boomed. Something heavy hit the roof behind her.

Jen jumped into nothingness.

8

The gaping chasm loomed below as she sailed through the air. *Too slow, I'm moving too slow.* Images and sounds assaulted her senses. The blast of a gun. Zeke rolling across the roof and bouncing to his feet. The beat of footsteps on the roof behind her. Mark aiming his rifle at her. Zeke's laugh as he rushed forward, waving his katana over his head. The edge of the roof barreling up to meet her.

Not going to make it.

Jen tucked her head and slammed into the rooftop inches from the edge. She tumbled forward a few revolutions and ended up flat on her back with her arms and legs splayed. Zeke stood over her. "You OK?" he yelled over the crack of another gunshot.

Jen took a deep breath and waited for the pain to come. She flexed her hands and bent her legs, but they seemed fine. Even her back wasn't complaining. "Looks like I got lucky."

Zeke stepped past her, swinging the katana. A head

rolled by. Zombies streamed over the edge of the hotel roof and most disappeared in the gap. A few leapt for the roof and missed, all except the one that Zeke had taken care of before it could do any damage.

She placed her hands flat on the roof and pushed. Mark reached for her right hand. "We can't stay here." He pulled and she rose to her feet.

Another zombie made it across, and Zeke dispatched it before it could gather itself.

Stuck in the middle of a zombie-infested city with no transportation. Got to get out of this shit and get to Atlanta where it's safe.

The deluge of zombies ended. Zeke kept his katana at the ready. "Why do you want to move? This position's pretty easy to defend."

"They know we're here," Mark said. "We're supposed to be observing, not engaging."

Jen cracked her neck. "I agree with Mark, but not because the zombies that ran off the roof know that we're here. I'm more concerned with how many zombies that we haven't seen know we're here."

"Come again?" Mark asked.

"How the hell did all those zombies know we were there? We made no noise. When we waved at the zombies on the tracks, there were no others in sight. So why would they rush the roof in a big group so suddenly?"

"That zombie that led the others," Zeke said. "It was like he spotted us and let the others know."

Mark put his hands on his hips. "Come on. You're not saying that they're communicating with each other, are you? They didn't even shriek like they used to."

"I agree with Zeke," Jen said. "I know it sounds insane,

but how many times in the past few weeks have we thought something couldn't happen, only to find out the impossible had become routine?"

She sighed. "We can talk about that later. We need to get to somewhere safe. Another rooftop. They're probably on their way up here now."

She went to the building door, turned the handle, and pushed it in. Stairs led down fifteen feet to another door. A zombie girl darted out from beneath the stairs and rushed Jen. She jumped backward out of the doorway and pulled the door closed with a loud click.

The zombie banged on the door.

A confused look crossed Zeke's face. "It's only one zombie. Why didn't you kill it?"

"I got sloppy and wasn't ready." She drew her axe.

The door clicked and opened into the building. Jen's heart skipped a beat. *What the hell?*

The zombie girl stood inside the doorway, her hand still on the door handle.

"What the fuck?" Mark said.

The zombie leapt for Jen, who slammed the axe into the base of its skull. Zeke finished it off with one slash.

"We're out of time." Jen hurried down the stairs and rushed into the hallway. She strained to pick up any sound beyond the rustling of Mark and Zeke behind her.

Pushing the door beneath an Exit sign, she entered the stairwell. Zeke eased the door closed and Jen held up a hand. She closed her eyes and listened.

"Nothing obvious," she whispered. "We can't get trapped in a stairwell, so whatever we run into, we fight through."

Mark stepped in front of her. "I go first and Zeke takes the rear."

She opened her mouth to argue, but remembered how she'd insisted that Doc stay in the middle of the group in Anchorage. "OK."

Mark kept his rifle pointed down the stairs as he took the steps at double time. Stopping at every floor, they listened for a few seconds, then continued.

When they reached the bottom of the stairwell, Mark pushed the door open, and they stepped into a coffee shop.

Undisturbed, everything lay in its place. Jen pointed to the front door, which had a picture window next to it. "Let's get on that street and the hell out of here. If those zombies were able to let others know we're here, it shouldn't be long before they show up."

Mark knelt next to the window and looked up and down the road. "Nothing I can see, but my angles aren't good here." He turned to Jen. "We need a rooftop that's not far away so we can signal the helicopter when it comes for pickup."

Jen bit her lip. "But it has to be far enough away so anything on this rooftop or the hotel's can't see us."

Mark looked at her and sighed. There was something different in his expression.

He's afraid. He could deal with an enemy that he knows. But if I'm right, then how much more don't we know about the zombies?

Mark pushed the door open and stepped onto the sidewalk. Jen crowded behind him. The street stood deserted.

They crept to the right, staying against the building, and surveyed the streets when they reached a convenience store on the corner. *Not a damn thing.*

"Where the hell are they all?" Jen asked.

Mark shook his head. "Not seeing any makes me more nervous than seeing a few."

Zeke pointed across the street. "There. That office building. Five stories and taller than any of the buildings on the block."

"Good," Jen said. "Need to get off the streets."

Zeke touched her arm. His eyes squinted and he cocked his head. "Listen," he whispered.

Jen froze and concentrated. Something in the distance. Soft, but getting louder fast. Reminded her of a cattle stampede in an old Western. *Shit.* "Horde."

She grabbed the convenience store's door handle and pulled, but it didn't budge. Mark yanked on the other door with the same result.

The stampede grew louder, the sound bouncing off the buildings.

"I can't even tell what direction it's coming from," Jen said. Heart pumping a mile a minute, she looked around for cover.

"No time to think about it," Mark said. "We have to make a break for the office building."

Her mouth dry, Jen nodded.

Mark gestured for them to follow, then streaked across the road and into a small parking lot next to the office building.

The thundering footsteps seemed to come from everywhere, building to a crescendo about to burst like a swollen dam.

Jen raced after Mark, with Zeke zipping past her.

Mark ducked in between two trucks and Jen dove in with him. He had taken a knee and gestured for Jen and Zeke to do the same.

Vibrations from the stampede traveled through the asphalt. A flash of movement caught Jen's eye and she looked out into the parking lot. A flood of zombies rushed by.

Her stomach fluttering and taking shallow breaths, she froze. *Don't give them a reason to look this way.*

The stampede seemed to never end. She had a fleeting thought that they were running circles around them and she was seeing the same zombies over and over. But the number began to trickle down. A few minutes later, the stragglers passed, their footsteps fading in the distance.

Mark put his hand out. Jen nodded. She wasn't moving anytime soon.

When another two minutes went by, she gave Mark a thumbs-up. He nodded, and she peered over the back of a truck.

Quiet. No movement. "I think we're OK," she whispered.

"I wonder where they were going," Zeke said.

Mark licked his lips. "They headed in the direction of the hotel."

"Oh, shit," Jen said. "We would've been overrun."

Mark straightened. "Let's get in the office building and out of sight."

They raced into the building, piling into the lobby.

"Wait," Jen said. She clicked the door's deadbolt into place. "Let's see if they're smart enough to pick a lock."

"We should clear the building and check all the doors and ground floor windows," Mark said.

"I'll take the second floor," Zeke said.

Jen frowned. "Maybe we should just stick together."

Zeke pulled his katana and gave it a practice swing. "This has been a boring mission. Betty and I could use a little fun."

Jen glanced at Mark. *Can you believe this guy?*

Mark gave her a slight shrug. "We'll meet you at the stairway on the second floor."

A half hour later, they pushed open the door to the roof

and stepped into the sunlight. Jen ducked and positioned herself at the southern edge. Not a zombie in sight. *Good.*

Mark waved her over. "We need to stay out of sight."

"This mission's shit," Zeke said. "Not one damn zombie in the building."

Jen sat down next to the ninja. "It's a good thing. How many zombies were in that horde that rumbled by us earlier? Think you could kill all of them?"

Zeke smiled. "Dunno, but it'd be a lot of fun to try."

Mark shook his head and sat on the roof, his back against the door.

TWO HOURS LATER, Jen was about to doze off when Zeke said, "Listen."

The thumping of helicopter rotors came closer, and Jen scrambled to her feet. "Where's it coming from?"

Zeke pointed south. "There."

The tiny helicopter grew larger and louder as it approached. It hovered a couple of blocks away. "They're over the hotel," Zeke said. "We need to get their attention."

He jumped and waved. "Over here," he screamed.

Mark tackled him and Jen put a hand over his mouth. "Just wave," she said, "but do it back from the edge of the roof where the helicopter can see you, but the zombies on the street can't."

Zeke looked at her with big eyes and nodded his head. Jen removed her hand.

Mark released Zeke and he stood, wiping off his ninja outfit. "We're OK. They didn't hear me over the rotor blades."

Something crashed below them, and Jen's breath

hitched. She inched toward the front of the building and peeked over the edge. The front door she'd secured had been smashed in and scores of zombies rushed in through the breach.

They'll be here any minute.

9

J en pulled her pistol. "They've broken into the building."

"Shit." Mark held his handgun with one hand and took his mace in the other. "We need that helicopter now."

It still hovered over the hotel. *What the hell is it doing?* Jen pointed the pistol in the air and fired a round. Damn thing didn't move. "Next time we make sure we get a radio."

The first zombie ran into the door to the roof.

Have to find someplace defensible.

More thumps from the door. It rattled in its frame.

"There." Mark pointed to the door.

Zeke's eyebrows lowered. "There what?"

"The raised rooftop entry. We can get on top."

"Brilliant." Jen ran to the side of the entry.

Mark laced his hands together. "You first, Zeke. Then Jen."

Zeke stepped on Mark's hands and pulled himself onto the roof. Mark boosted Jen, and she grabbed Zeke's outstretched hand.

The door burst open and zombies poured onto the roof, rushing away from them. Jen and Zeke reached down, each taking one of Mark's hands, and strained to pull him up. One of the zombies turned and rushed for Mark. It grabbed for his dangling leg and Mark lashed out with his foot, bashing the zombie's head with his boot heel. Jen and Zeke dug in, the tendons in Zeke's neck standing out. Teeth gritted, Mark rolled onto the roof on his stomach.

Jen bent over, hands on her knees, panting.

Zeke slashed at the zombies trying to climb onto their perch. Jen aimed and fired at their heads while Mark swung his mace in great arcs to keep them back.

Even though they climbed and groped at the humans, the zombies uttered no sound. *Not even a damn grunt. Creepy shit.*

The thump of helicopter rotors caught Jen's attention. Their rescuers headed their way.

"It's coming," she yelled.

The draft from the rotor blades nearly blew Jen over. She emptied her magazine and reloaded.

A rope lowered from the chopper. "Jen goes first," Mark yelled.

She shook her head and Mark glared, then pointed to the rope.

The zombies were stacking up, and one grabbed Mark's pant leg, throwing him off balance. His arms windmilled as he tipped toward the ravenous horde. Jen grabbed his arm and Zeke sliced through the zombie's arm. With Jen's help, Mark righted himself. "Go now," he yelled, and clubbed a hairy, bearded zombie on the temple. "The longer you take, the longer before I can get out of here."

Jen grabbed the rope and looked up at the soldier visible

in the helicopter's door. He made a wind up gesture and she rose to the helicopter.

It had probably taken only a minute to get there, but still seemed too slow. Mark and Zeke swung and shot, and chopped and hacked at the undead closing in on them.

Jen crouched next to the soldier and he pointed at the seat. She shook her head and pulled the rifle off her shoulder. Propping it against the door, she aimed at the head of a zombie reaching out for Zeke while he dealt with another one. Holding her breath, she pulled the trigger and the back of the zombie's head blew out.

The rope reached Mark and Zeke. Mark nudged Zeke and nodded to the rope. Zeke cleared his side of the raised rooftop entry and grabbed the rope. Jen concentrated on keeping the zombies from climbing up behind Mark. Without taking time to control her breathing, she killed a half dozen zombies before she missed. She pulled the trigger and nothing happened. The action was open. *Shit. Empty.*

She scrambled to grab a fresh magazine. The zombie she'd missed had climbed up behind Mark. "Mark. Behind you," she screamed.

Mark's attention stayed on the horde before him. Barely keeping them back, he'd stopped using his pistol and battered them with his mace.

Jen ejected the empty magazine and slammed the new one in. Zeke climbed in the helicopter beside her and aimed his rifle downward.

Jen jacked a round into the chamber. The zombie grabbed Mark's collar and pulled him backward.

Jen shot and the zombie fell into the horde below. With that small pause, the undead in front of Mark pulled themselves up.

Zeke killed them as fast as they came. Jen continued raining down lead on the creatures behind Mark. Still a few got through, but Mark made quick work of them with the mace.

Mark stumbled. *He has to be exhausted.*

The rope dangled behind him. *He doesn't see it.*

She yelled, "Mark. The rope."

Zeke aimed his rifle. "I've got this." He slowly squeezed the trigger. The bullet hit right behind Mark.

Mark jumped and glanced behind him. Grabbing the rope, he swung the mace wildly. The damn zombies were too close to him. Jen couldn't risk hitting him.

Mark bashed and kicked as he rose. Dozens of zombies had made it to the entry roof and all reached for him. The helicopter ascended and pulled Mark out of the horde's reach. He plopped onto the floor a minute later.

The soldier said something into his mic and the helicopter flew toward base.

HOWELL STOOD by a Humvee several yards from the helipad. Jen jumped out and stumbled over to him. "Hope you don't expect us to tip you for these rides."

Howell grinned. "They're on the house."

The helicopter rotors slowed as Mark and Zeke walked up.

"Heard you folks had your hands full out there," Howell said.

"You could say that." Mark cracked his neck. "All I want right now is a hot shower, some chow, and a nap. What do you say, Zeke?"

Zeke looked at Mark as if he had grown another head.

"I'm just getting started." He smiled at Howell. "But this last mission was freaking epic."

Jen opened the Humvee door. "Let's get back to the rooms, Mr. Epic."

Five minutes later, they piled out at Headquarters. Howell lowered his window. "Colonel's gonna want to debrief you."

"I'll keep my briefs on, if you don't mind," Jen said. "Colonel or no colonel."

Mark ignored her. "Why does he need a debriefing? Jen's working for Dr. Cartwright."

Howell shrugged. "His base. His rules."

"How did he become in charge of this base, anyway?" Mark said. "I've never seen an Army officer in command of an Air Force base."

Howell scratched his chin. "The wing commander was killed in the first horde attack. That was the day after Colonel Butler arrived. Guess the brass figured he was already here, so they might as well give him the command."

"Sounds convenient," Mark said. "For Butler."

Howell studied Mark's face, then said, "Not sure I'd call it that. Anyway, I arrived a couple days later. Most of the Air Force folks are gone. All except a few flight line personnel."

He closed the window halfway, then turned back to Jen. "Colonel's on a post inspection for the next forty minutes, so you should be ready for the debrief by then." He drove off.

"That gives you enough time to conference with Dr. Cartwright," Zeke said.

Mark slapped Zeke's back. "Not a bad idea. Get the findings to Cartwright now. Who knows what Butler may do? In fact, I wouldn't tell him shit. Just say the zombies acted the same."

"That's a hell of a dangerous game to play," Jen said.

"Not as dangerous as trusting Butler," Mark said. "Have you already forgotten how he left us in Anchorage to die?"

"But what about the innocent soldiers?" Jen asked. "Shouldn't they know?"

Mark's eyes narrowed. She'd hit a sore spot. "How will we turn on the video conferencing equipment?"

"Leave that to me," Zeke said. "I helped set up audiovisual equipment in high school."

Jen grinned. "Should've known."

Zeke led the way to the room. He walked in, flipped a switch on a console on the table, then pushed a button. The TV came on but remained blank until the word *Connecting* displayed.

"Can't wait to get the hell out of here," Jen said.

Mark leaned into the hallway and peered up and down the passage before closing the door.

The monitor filled with Dr. Cartwright's upper body, leaning on a desk. She peered over her glasses, a curt expression pasted on her face. "Jen. What do you have for me?"

Jen licked her lips. How much should she tell her?

In the end she told her everything: their mission and how the zombies seemed to communicate without speaking, how they suspected that the zombies that turned without being bitten seemed smarter than the others.

Cartwright took her glasses off and let them dangle from the chain looped around her neck. "We have some specimens here, but all have been bitten. Our strict protocols have kept the newly dead from rising. We may have to make some exceptions."

She frowned. "What did you call them again? Leaders and what?"

"Drones," Jen said. "Leaders and drones."

"Can we leave this place now?" Mark asked. "She's given you the information you need."

The door burst open and Butler marched in. "How dare you start a debrief without me?"

Howell strode in and closed the door behind him.

"Colonel Butler," Dr. Cartwright said. "You will be given information as I see fit. Jen works for me, not you."

"I suppose I'll be rid of her now that she's reported back to you."

Jen stood. *I can't believe I'm doing this, but there's more to learn here and I'm in the best position to learn it. Besides, Butler wants us gone too badly. He's up to something.* "I'm staying for a while longer. I believe there's more to learn about the new zombie behaviors." She shrugged. "It could end up meaning nothing in the long run, but it could also be a game-changer in this war. In the memory of my father and Doc, and so many others, I have to risk staying in the field for this."

10

B utler's face flushed. "What the hell do you mean you're staying? The deal was a week."

Jen clenched her fists. *I'd love to kick this asshole in the nuts...if he had any.*

Mark stepped between Butler and Jen, and Zeke pressed in on her side.

"There's no need to shout." Cartwright's face had the same placid expression as if she were placing a dinner order.

Butler stopped in front of Mark and turned toward the monitor. "I've got the defense of the United States on my shoulders, and I don't have the time to babysit civilians."

"Babysit?" Jen leaned around Mark to glower at Butler. "Listen, Colonel Butthead. We can take care of ourselves."

"Really?" Butler sneered. "And who had to be airlifted just today before they were overrun?"

Mark's jaw muscles tightened and Jen gently pulled him to her side. Butler glared down at her.

"So when you airlift your own troops, do you consider it babysitting?" Jen asked.

Butler sputtered, "They're soldiers. They're supposed to be supported."

Cartwright cleared her throat and everyone's attention shifted to her.

"So you're saying that airlifting assets from the field is support?" Cartwright gave a slight smile. "And not babysitting?"

Butler puffed his chest. "Our agreement was for these civilians to stay for a week. The week is up and they need to leave."

"But there's more work to be done," Cartwright said. "I'm proud and thankful that Jen has volunteered to stay and follow up on her recent findings."

"What findings?" Butler asked. "And why wasn't I informed?"

Cartwright gestured to the monitor. "Jen?"

Jen licked her lips, but her mouth had gone dry. "The zombies"—she gave a slight shake of her head—"or the virus, have evolved. We observed behavior that indicates the zombies' cognitive abilities have increased."

"Cut with all the flowery language and tell me what you saw."

"A zombie opened a door that was latched."

Butler stared at her for a moment, then chuckled. "Are you shitting me? Those meat bags are dumb as shit."

"I know what I saw," Jen said.

Mark thrust his jaw forward. "I saw it, too."

"Me, too," Zeke said.

"Look," Butler said. "Maybe one of them opened a door, but I'll bet it was already partly open and the damn thing stumbled into it at the right angle and knocked it open." He looked at Cartwright. "You're a scientist. Don't you have to have more evidence? A bigger number of them?"

"A larger sampling size?" Cartwright steepled her fingers before her. "That's a good point, Colonel."

Butler put his hands on his hips and nodded. The red was receding from his face. "That's what I mean. I'm glad someone here has some sense."

Jen smiled. "Then we agree."

"About what?" Butler growled.

"We need a larger sample size. Of course, that means we need more observation, and in order to do that, we'll have to stay here for a while longer."

"What?" Butler said. "No."

"I'm briefing General Lewis on our status in about an hour," Cartwright said. "I'll pass on that Jen and her team are staying, and that you agree."

Butler's lips pressed together, drawing a thin line across his face. He closed his eyes and his nostrils flared, then he took a deep breath and exhaled. "Agreed."

He opened his eyes and lowered his brow, staring at Cartwright. "But I will be briefed on all activities. This team will not leave this base without either me or Sergeant Howell knowing where they're going, what they're doing, and when they'll return."

Fat chance, asshole. Jen waited for Cartwright to knock him down to size.

Cartwright stared at the monitor then reached forward, her hand disappearing below the picture. "Agreed." The connection closed.

What the Holy Hell?

Butler scowled. "Give your outside itineraries to Sergeant Howell and coordinate all activities with him."

He marched toward the door and stopped when he stepped into the hallway. He glanced over his shoulder. "And this room is off-limits. You will not have any communication with Dr. Cartwright unless and until I authorize it."

He disappeared down the hall, with Howell following in his wake.

Jen kicked a chair, sending it slamming into the wall. "That asshole. What the hell does he hope to get from all this bullshit?"

"He's hiding something," Zeke said.

"What?" Jen asked.

Mark nodded. "I agree with Zeke. He is hiding something and he doesn't want it to get out. I'll bet the brass would replace him if they knew, and that's what he's trying to avoid."

"So we've got an asshole colonel who's supposed to be trying to save the world, but he's doing something underhanded?"

Zeke sat on the conference table. "He's an asshole all right, but I think in his mind he's a patriot that will do anything he thinks he needs to do for his country."

"Great," Jen mumbled.

Mark clapped his hands together. "I'm pretty hungry and you two smell like zombie shit. How about we clean up and get something to eat?"

Thirty minutes later they sat at a corner table in the chow hall.

Jen made a face when she swallowed a mouthful of mashed potatoes. They had an off taste. *Probably dehydrated.* "We should target different sections of the city each time we go out."

"Maybe we can get hold of some night vision gear and go out at night," Mark said. "Unless they can see in the dark, it'd give us a clear advantage."

Zeke pushed his chair back and stood. Jen looked up. "You leaving?"

Zeke ignored her and walked toward the exit door for the serving line. Grant walked out, holding a tray.

"Grant," Zeke called.

Grant's gaze snapped to Zeke, and his eyes grew wide. He glanced at a table of soldiers to his right. Several of them had stopped eating and turned to look at him.

Grant ignored Zeke and continued toward the soldiers' table.

Zeke put a hand on Grant's arm. "Hey, Grant."

Grant dropped his tray, the dishes cracking and the food splattering as it hit the floor.

"Now look what you've done," Grant roared.

Zeke stepped back, his mouth working like a fish out of water. "Sorry. Didn't mean to startle you."

Grant grabbed Zeke by the front of his costume. "Startle? You knocked my tray down."

Mark jumped to his feet and took a couple of steps toward Zeke.

More and more heads turned to witness the argument. The table of soldiers had all turned and watched with keen interest.

Grant grabbed Zeke's hands and used them to mimic a push. "This. This is what you did. Why? What the hell do you want?"

"I—I was going to invite you to join us." Zeke gestured to the table where Jen sat. Her mouth hung open. *What the hell's wrong with Grant?*

"You're all civilians," Grant yelled. "I'm going to sit with my battle buddies. I don't have time for you."

Zeke turned back to the table. Jen's heart broke. Zeke looked crushed. Mark walked Zeke back to the table.

"It's OK," Jen said. "He's always been an asshole to you. That's all he is. Now that he's back with the military and doesn't need us to save his ass, we see his true colors."

Mark patted Zeke's back. "I should've kicked that guy's ass a long time ago."

Zeke's shocked face slowly transformed and he smiled.

Jen's eyes narrowed. "What the hell's wrong with you?"

"Grant's OK," Zeke said. "He's still our friend."

"What do you mean?" Mark asked.

Zeke put his closed left hand to his chest and looked around. With a satisfied grin, he turned his hand palm up and opened it, revealing a folded slip of paper.

11

J en looked up and down the hallway, then closed the door to her room. "So what's Grant's note say?"

Zeke unfolded the paper and squinted. "You're being watched by everyone. Colonel's orders. I need to speak to Jen. Tonight behind the base motor pool two blocks to the west of Headquarters at ten o'clock."

"Who'd've taken Grant as a James Bond type?" Jen said.

Mark rubbed his face. "Could be a trap."

"No." Zeke handed the paper to Jen. "Grant's a good guy."

Jen read the message and tore it up. "Why do you say he's a good guy? He gave you a lot of shit in Anchorage."

Zeke shrugged. "He was scared. But he came through for us when we needed him, didn't he?"

Jen walked into the bathroom, dropped the torn pieces of paper into the toilet, and flushed it.

"He did come through in Anchorage and Klawock," Mark said. "I know I'd be dead if not for him." He pointed at Jen. "You, too."

Jen pursed her lips. *Maybe Grant knows what the hell's*

going on around here. "I think it's worth the chance. I'm going."

AT NINE O'CLOCK, Jen stood in the empty lobby with Mark and Zeke.

"Let's go over it one more time," she said. "At nine thirty, you both leave your rooms and head in opposite directions, and I'll scoot out at nine forty."

"So you're just going to walk out the front door?" Mark asked.

Jen smirked. "You know me better than that, but I'm not telling you how I'm leaving. Better that you don't know."

"This is going to be epic," Zeke said. "I'll head to the east, then I'll melt into the shadows and tail anyone that's following me."

"Don't get caught," Mark said.

"Shit." Zeke smiled. "I made it around that mall in Anchorage and never got caught. I've got a much bigger playground here."

Jen laughed. "I'll talk to you both in the morning. No sense making anyone suspicious by getting together late at night."

"OK." Zeke walked down the hall that led to his room.

Mark stood silent for a moment, staring at Jen. "Be careful. I know you can take care of yourself, but if you see or hear anything that's not right when you get there, get the hell out. Grant's a soldier, and he may prize that more than the bond we all share from survival."

Jen gave Mark a hug, and he seemed taken aback. After a minute, he put his arms around her and squeezed gently, then broke the hug.

"Remember, anything unusual and you get out of there." He turned and took the hallway that led to his room.

Jen called after him. "OK, big brother. I will."

She whistled and sauntered across the lobby and into the hallway leading to the chow hall.

As she'd hoped, it was empty. She opened the cold case and pulled a soda out. Popping it open, she sat at the table closest to the women's rest room. The clock on the wall read nine ten p.m.

She wasn't worried about a trap. After all, if Grant had set her up, he knew she'd get to him eventually. *And he wants to keep his balls.*

A pair of soldiers walked by in the hallway, talking. Neither paid her any attention.

Did Grant know what Butler was hiding? Or maybe there was something else, something important enough for him to risk the meeting.

At nine thirty, she tipped the soda can, downing the last of the drink. She stood, crushed the can, and shot it like a basketball into a trash can ten feet away. She raised her arms when it went in. "Score."

No one had come into the chow hall the whole time she'd been there. She looked around at the walls, vents, and light fixtures, searching for anything that looked like a camera. *Damn, I'm really getting paranoid.*

The clock said nine thirty-five. She pushed the ladies' room door open and walked in. After checking the stalls to make sure they were empty, she unlatched the window and waited.

When her watch flashed nine forty, she tip toed to the door and hit the light switch, plunging the bathroom into darkness. A soft glow from the frosted window guided her there, and she slid it up a quarter inch at a time, praying it made no noise.

She stuck her head out. No movement. Nothing but crickets and the sound of an engine starting in the distance.

A slight breeze washed over Jen as she climbed through the window and lowered herself to the ground. Praying no one would enter the bathroom while she was gone, she crouched and snuck to the edge of the building.

All was quiet, so she darted across the grass to the next building and slipped between it and a warehouse. Across the next road stood a darkened field. Down the road to her left, light spilled out of a short, one-story building, and the sound of metal hitting metal echoed from it. Voices spoke every minute or so, but no one came out.

She'd have to make it across the street and across the field without being seen. *Got to go. Grant may not wait if I don't show up on time.*

She dashed across the road, her footsteps sounding as loud as gunshots to her. They muffled when she hit the grass. She glanced left at the occupied building, but no one ran out pointing at her and calling for help. *Or shooting.*

Jen raced to the back of a shadowy building and crouched beside it, her heart racing.

Standing hunched over, she crept to the side of the building and paused to listen for any movement. A helicopter rose in the distance, its lights heading away from base.

She peered around the side of the building. Pools of light from the street lamps splashed onto the asphalt.

Taking time to place each foot solidly on the ground so as not to crunch the gravel, she made her way to the front.

The motor pool stood across the street, one of its overhead doors open and looking like a huge, dark mouth waiting for someone to enter so it could close and swallow them.

Jen sprinted across the road, her boots scuffing on the asphalt. The sound echoed off the buildings.

She slipped inside the door and hugged the wall. As her eyes got used to the darkness, shadows emerged. A large one several feet in front of her had the outline of a truck. Other lumps to her left could've been anything.

She took a deep breath. "Grant?"

She cringed. Even though she'd spoken in a near whisper, it sounded like a shout in the stillness.

"Grant. You there?"

A rustle from deep in the garage put her in a defensive crouch. Without thinking, her axe appeared in her hand.

"Jen?" Grant whispered.

"Over here."

A shadow detached from the back and moved toward her. "Where?" Grant asked.

"Keep coming straight forward."

The shadow stopped in front of her, its breathing shallow and fast. A hand touched her chest.

"Hey," Jen said. "Watch it with that. You didn't bring me out here just to cop a feel, did you?"

"No. No. Oh, God. I didn't mean it. I was just trying to figure out where you were."

"Relax, soldier boy. I know it was an accident. You should, too. After all, your hand's still attached to your arm."

Grant chuckled. "Always a hot shit."

"Enough old home days," Jen said. "What have you got for me?"

"Like I wrote. Everyone's watching you. They're watching me some, too, because I came in with you. It's obvious they don't totally trust me yet."

"So what?"

"Something's not right here," Grant said. "I heard you're staying. I wanted to warn you to go. I don't think you're safe here. Hell, I don't think I'm safe here."

Jen scoffed. "Out in the middle of nowhere with millions of zombies probably on their way? What's not to feel safe about?"

"Not the zombies. Butler. There's something going on at Area 51."

"What?" Jen asked. "What's going on?"

Headlights swung around a corner and bathed them in LED light for a moment. Grant grabbed Jen's arm and pulled her behind the truck. "Shit. It's them."

The large truck rumbled by, the throaty roar of its engine fading into the distance.

Grant's heavy breathing was the only sound remaining.

"I think we're OK," Jen said.

Grant stood. "We better leave."

"Drag me all the way out here and leave me hanging?" Jen said. "Bullshit. You're not going anywhere until I hear what you have to say."

A streetlight's beam fell across half of Grant's face. He licked his lips. "Area 51. Those trucks, they're what's wrong."

"What trucks?" Jen pointed to the street. "You mean that one that just passed?"

Grant nodded. "My job is to drive trucks, and every day at three a.m. I bring one to the supply building on the flight line. It gets loaded with supplies."

"What kind of supplies?"

"Don't know. I'm supposed to sit in the truck and wait for it to be loaded. Once it is, a sergeant tells me I'm good to go, and I drive to Area 51."

Jen folded her arms. "What's in there?"

Grant shrugged. "I back into the loading bay and turn it off. There's always an empty truck parked there. I take that one back to the supply building."

"Come on, Grant. You brought me all the way the hell out here for that?"

He shook his head. "The trucks at night—like the one that just passed—are different."

"Different how?"

"They told me to drive one of them once when the regular driver was on sick call. They brought me to a warehouse on the edge of the base, told me to drive the truck to Area 51 as normal and bring back the unloaded truck.

"I backed into the loading dock," Grant said, "and there was no one around. I shut off the engine and had just opened the door when it happened."

"You're really stretching this out," Jen said. "What the hell happened?"

"Something in the back of the truck banged on the side."

Jen frowned. "Loose cargo."

"No. The truck had been stopped for a minute, and it was the first time I'd heard anything. I walked to the other truck and heard it from the back of the first truck again. There was someone or something moving in the back of that truck."

"Why didn't you open the back and see?"

Grant shivered. "I had this feeling of being watched. No one in sight, but I could've sworn someone had eyes on me. I jumped into that other truck and lit out of there."

Another set of lights came down the road. The vehicle stopped under a streetlight. "An MP truck," Grant said.

The truck's passenger shined a spotlight into the building behind the streetlight.

"Shit," Jen said. "We've got to get out of here."

"Come on. There's a back door."

Jen followed Grant into the cool night air. The spotlight shined through the motor pool's windows. They waited for the truck to move on, then Jen let out a breath. "So why are you telling me all this? What am I going to do about it?"

"You need to leave. But you can tell Dr. Cartwright what I told you. Something is going on and it's tied to Butler. No one talks about it. They go all quiet and ignore you if you mention it."

Jen bit her lower lip. Area 51 had tripped her radar the minute she'd seen it. Why an armed guard? The security door and scanner should be enough protection for a communications building. And why the armed soldiers lining the hallway? And the secret deliveries?

"Jen?"

She broke away from her thoughts. "I'll talk to Cartwright, but I can't leave yet. Not only is there more to do, but it'd look suspicious if I left just after I said I needed to stay."

"Then watch your back." Grant took a few steps from the building and looked both ways. "We better get out of here before the MPs come back. Take care of yourself." He slipped off into the shadows.

SOMEONE BANGED on Jen's door. She sprung from bed and reached for her axe.

"Miss Reed. Colonel Butler wants to see you."

Jen put her hand on her chest, afraid her heart would burst from it. "Hold on."

Throwing a robe on, she noted the five a.m. time on the digital clock.

She jerked the door open. An MP stood in the hallway.

"Five in the morning?" she said. "Who the hell gets up at five in the freaking morning?"

"Sorry, ma'am." He looked anything but sorry. "Colonel Butler wants to see you now." His eyes dipped to her cleavage and Jen pulled the robe tighter around herself.

"Give me a minute." She closed the door and damn near jumped into her clothes. Opening the door, she pushed past the MP. "Let's go."

Butler sat behind a desk, a cup of black coffee against his lips. He took a sip and put the cup down. "Miss Reed. Got something for you. In light of our mutual goal of getting you and your civvie friends out of here, I'm taking you out this morning for some observing."

Jen took a seat and swung one leg over the side. Butler's jaw tightened. *Good.*

"I'm game. Another roundup?"

"Not for you," Butler said. "We'll drop you and your friends off on our way to a roundup."

"No."

Butler's eyebrows shot up. "No? You said no to me?"

"Last time we did that the chopper was too far off when we ran into trouble."

Butler shrugged. "We'll drop you off only a block or two from the roundup. You'll have all the firepower close by."

Jen scowled. She couldn't say no and not seem unreasonable.

"I'll even throw your friend, Specialist Grant, in. I'll bet you two have lots to talk about."

Jen's heart skipped a beat. Did he know?

Butler sat back in his chair and laced his fingers behind his head. "Been a while since you've talked, no?"

Son of a bitch does know.

Change the subject back. "It's a deal," she said. "But we get a radio."

Butler smiled. "That'll work. You and your team need to be in the lobby at oh-six-thirty hours. Sergeant Howell will shuttle you to the helicopter."

Jen gave him a curt nod and walked out.

TWO HOURS LATER, Jen jumped onto the roof of an office building. Mark, Grant, and Zeke hopped off the Blackhawk and landed next to her. The pilot waved and took off.

Jen surveyed the roof. "Zeke, wanna check out that door?"

Zeke popped her a salute and jogged to the door.

"Why am I here?" Grant asked.

Jen went to one knee and pulled Grant with her. "Butler knows we met. He offered to have you come with us. I had no other way to warn you that he knows."

"So you two were caught last night?" Mark turned his gaze on Jen. "Why didn't you tell us when you came to get us this morning?"

"We weren't caught last night," Jen said. "At least no one confronted us last night."

Zeke jerked a thumb over his shoulder. "Door's secure as long as we don't have a horde storm it, or run into one of those smart zombies."

The radio on Jen's belt squawked. "Command One to all units. Commence firing."

Gunfire broke out nearby. Jen shaded her eyes and looked toward the sound. Sure enough, the Blackhawk had landed on a building four blocks away.

"Let's get observing." She walked to the edge of the roof overlooking West Main Avenue.

Mark joined her. "I'd like to get this observing shit done and get out of here. I feel better that the zombies haven't taken over the rest of the country, but I still need to check on my family."

"I'm with you," Jen said. "But if we find something that helps Cartwright and the CDC crack this thing, your family may never be in danger."

Deserted, the street reminded Jen of one of those Hollywood end-of-the-world movies.

Mark pointed to their right. "I'll go watch this side."

"Good idea," Jen said. "Grant, why don't you take the side across the roof, and Zeke, take the last one."

Grant nodded and jogged to his post.

I remember when he wanted to be in charge back in Anchorage. I like him better now.

Zeke stood there for a moment. "Is this all we're going to do? Just stand up here?"

"That's the plan. Unless something goes to shit."

He huffed and lumbered to his side of the building. Jen peered back onto the street. It hadn't changed.

"Command One to all units. Zulus have broken through. Use all available firepower."

Explosions echoed down the streets, and black smoke rose above the buildings, blocking the helicopter from view. *What the hell?*

She looked at Mark, who turned toward her and shrugged. Zeke danced and clapped. Grant had taken a knee and watched the smoke with a frown.

Jen pointed at each of them in turn. Every one of them scanned their side of the building and shook their head. *We're not going to see shit here. All the zombies are corralled and being wiped out.*

"Command One to all units. Cease fire. I repeat, cease fire. Let the smoke clear so we can assess the situation."

The smoke had drifted almost to Jen's position. The acrid sulfur-laden cloud probed her nostrils and caused her to sneeze. She shoved her face into the crook of her arm.

Another helicopter swooped in overhead. Mark ran over. "That's an Apache Longbow and it's armed for bear."

The smoke swirled beneath the Apache's spinning blades.

"Echo One to Command One."

"Go, Echo One."

"The smoke's cleared on our position, east building. Zulus are escaping down side street, heading for West Main Avenue."

"Roger, Echo One. Hotel Three, do you copy?"

"Copy."

The Apache swooped past Butler's position and descended until it disappeared behind the building.

"Hotel Three to command. We have eyes on Zulus. They've hit West Main Avenue and are heading west."

A horde dashed out from behind the building and flowed Jen's way. *If they keep their course, they'll pass right by us.*

"Command One to Hotel Three. Engage. Command One to Hotel One."

Explosions came from the other side of the building. The horde kept a straight course.

A Blackhawk swept in from the west and fired on the horde. Dozens of zombies fell in the street.

Movement on a building across the street caught Jen's eye. A zombie stood on the roof like a statue, staring at the oncoming horde.

"Hotel Three to Command One. Have engaged targets.

Be advised they're splitting up and finding cover in buildings."

"Holy shit," Mark said. "They are taking cover. No leaders, they're just going."

Jen pointed at a group disappearing into a movie theater on the other side of the street. "And they're splitting up evenly. What the hell?" *The zombie on the roof.*

Jen's gaze snapped to the roof. The zombie stood there, expressionless, its yellow eyes boring into hers.

13

Z eke raced over. "A bunch of undead just ran into this building."

"Shit." Jen waved Grant over. "We need to watch that damn door."

"Command One to Hotel One and Three. Disengage."

"Roger, Command One. Hotel One Disengaging."

"Hotel Three disengaged."

Grant joined them. "What's up?"

"We may be getting company," Mark said. "Zombies have entered this building."

"How many?"

Zeke wrinkled his nose. "I lost count. They were coming in too fast."

"Then make an educated guess," Mark said.

Zeke closed his eyes and held a finger up. Mark looked at Jen and rolled his eyes.

"Maybe fifty, but could be as much as a hundred," Zeke said.

"Command One to Alpha One. Target grids Victor Tango Zulu eight to fourteen."

"Oh, shit," Mark said. "We need to get out of here."

"What?" Jen asked. "What is it?"

Mark sprinted for the door. "When they talk about targeting, they're talking artillery. And since all the zombies are in our area..."

"Command One to Alpha One. Commence firing."

Mark grabbed Jen's arm. "Come on, Zeke."

Explosions on the street rattled the building. Jen lost her footing on the vibrating roof, but Mark kept her upright.

Grant had the door open and they all ducked inside. Mark let go of Jen and whipped out his flashlight. "The zombies went into the buildings, so Butler's going to destroy the buildings to take them out."

He shined the light on a door to the stairway. "Grant, take point."

"Butler knows we're here," Jen said.

Mark pointed at her. "Exactly."

Grant had his flashlight out and entered the stairs. "Zeke, you're next."

The building rocked, and Jen fell backward into a wall. Dust and debris fell from the ceiling.

Butler's going to raze these damn buildings to the ground. If he can't get us to leave, he'll just kill us and claim the zombies got us. The asshole.

Jen ran onto the stairs, with Mark behind her. She drew her pistol and followed Zeke. Grant had already made it to the first landing.

"Don't get too far ahead," Mark called out.

Grant waited, peering down the stairs. Just as Jen reached the landing, he looked up, his eyes wide. "They're coming. Three floors down."

Another blast hit the building. This time Jen kept her balance, but just barely.

She opened the door to a hallway and shooed the others in. Closing the door, she pushed past the others and opened the first door she found.

A copier room. Several plotters and printers stood against a wall, while metal cabinets lined another. She waved the others over. "Plenty of room in here."

Mark was the last in and closed the door. "Everyone in the corner."

They set up shoulder to shoulder, firearms aimed at the door. Jen peeked out the window next to her. The movie theater on the other side of the intersection was gone, and in its place lay an enormous pile of rubble. Across the street, the building where she'd seen the leader had lost its top two floors. Flames licked its sides. Down the road, the smoke was so thick, she couldn't see crap, but the chunks of wood and stone in the road gave her a clue to what she'd find there.

Another strike on their building hit below them.

"Command One to Alpha Two. Zero in on coordinates given to Alpha One and let go with everything you have. I don't want a building left standing in that area."

"Roger, Command One."

Jen keyed the radio. "Jen Reed to Command One. Come in."

No answer.

"Jen Reed to any unit. Please respond."

"Echo Three to Control. Northeast perimeter is secure."

"Control to Echo Three. Copy."

"Dammit. This is Jen Reed. We're in the area you're about to bomb. Cease fire."

"Alpha One to Command One. Coordinates input."

Jen sprung to her feet. "Fucking radio isn't transmitting.

Either we go now or we end up buried under this damn thing."

Grant cracked the door open. "All clear." He turned around. "I'm with Jen. At least we have a chance with the zombies."

"OK," Mark said. "Let's get back on the stairs, same setup with Grant at point. We don't stop. If we hit a horde, we fight our way through it or die."

Grant flung the door open and darted down the stairs, with Zeke on his heels. Jen entered the stairwell and glanced above. Two zombies had turned and headed their way. She nudged Mark and took a shot at one of the zombies just as the building took a hit. *Shit.*

Mark took out both zombies with head shots, but missed one on his first try.

"You're still handy to have around," she said.

He gave her a little push. "Go."

Grant and Zeke had made it to the next landing. Holding onto the rail, Jen took the stairs two at a time. Grant and Zeke continued pulling away and she picked up her pace. *Don't want to get separated.*

Her breath came in ragged gasps by the time they reached the third floor and the building took another hit. Somewhere in the darkness the stressed structure emitted a low groan.

Grant and Zeke stopped halfway down to the second floor. They had their rifles up and firing. A flood of zombies ran up the stairs. Jen took out several, but even with all of them shooting, there were too many targets. *Fifty zombies? More like a couple hundred.*

Grant and Zeke backed up until they stood on the landing with the others.

"No way we can take them all," Grant yelled.

Another barrage hit the building, knocking down several zombies. Pieces of wall fell on the stairs.

Mark opened the hallway door. "In here."

"What the hell?" Jen said. "We'll be trapped there."

"We'll take the stairs on the other side," Mark said.

"How do you know there are stairs on that side?"

He pointed to a sign on the wall for emergency evacuation procedures. *Sure enough.*

Jen raced down the hallway, a stitch in her side. She reached the other stairway door, readied her pistol, and shoved the door open.

Nothing.

She waved the others over. "It's clear."

Zeke and Grant sprinted to her, while Mark closed the door and joined them. "Let's hope there's not a leader with them."

Grant hesitated. "Where do we go when we get to the first floor?"

"What?" Zeke asked.

"Where do we go?" Grant repeated. "We can't stay in the building or we'll be buried, and we can't go outside with the shells hitting out there and buildings collapsing into the street."

"Shit," Jen said.

Zeke clapped his hands together. "I know. The basement."

"Are you fucking crazy?" Grant yelled.

"We'll be crushed down there," Jen said.

"Not if we take the sewers out of here." Zeke smiled.

Grant planted his hands on his hips. "How the hell do you know there's a sewer?"

"While all of you were asleep last night, I found a computer in an office, pulled up the internet, and read everything I could about this city." He pointed to his head. "A good ninja gathers all the information about the enemy and the battlefield that he can."

Mark laughed. "You're a genius."

Grant clapped Zeke on the shoulder. "Let's go, buddy." He raced down the stairs. Zeke gave Jen a thumbs-up and followed.

Jen reached the first floor just as Grant opened the door to the basement stairway. He shined his light down it. "Dreary looking."

"Not as dreary as it'll look when the building comes down," Mark said.

Another hit shook the building. Jen braced herself and stayed on her feet. The hits were coming every minute or so.

Two more strikes came moments apart—one not far above them and one in the street.

"Down," Mark yelled.

Something knocked Jen off her feet and onto her back. Her pistol skittered across the floor.

Her reflexes kicked in and she put her hands out in front of her just as a thirty-something zombie in a shredded business pantsuit landed on top of her. It opened its mouth and snapped its jaws.

Jen coughed at the smell. It had been over a week since she'd been hit with that stench.

A shot went off close by, and the side of the zombie's head exploded, spraying blood and bone across the floor. *And on my shirt.* Jen rolled the corpse off her and grabbed Mark's outstretched hand. "Thanks for the save."

Mark handed her pistol over. "Let's go."

Zeke appeared at the door. "What happened? We heard a gunshot."

Jen waved him back. "We're OK." She brushed past him and stood at the top of the stairway. Pulling her flashlight out, she turned it on then shined it down the stairs.

Musty and narrow, the concrete stairway went ten feet down, then took a ninety-degree angle to the left.

"Where's Grant?" Jen asked.

Zeke stood behind her. "Bottom of the stairs."

Mark pulled the door closed. "You go first, Zeke. You know the way."

They joined Grant at the bottom. He and Zeke shined their flashlight beams across a large basement. Shelves jutted out from the walls on one side, while boxes were stacked on another.

"Let's split up and find the damn sewer entrance," Jen said. "I'll go straight. Zeke and Grant, can you take the right side and check around those shelves?"

They spread out and approached the shelves.

Jen looked at Mark. "The left work for you?"

He grunted and nodded. "Keep your eyes open. If you see anything, sound out."

Jen swung her beam back and forth in front of her and eased forward. They had to get out of there fast, but it wasn't the time to take chances either. The strikes on the building were muffled down there, but it wouldn't be that way for long.

Zeke and Grant talked as they wound through the shelves. Mark moved boxes around, but otherwise stayed silent.

Jen reached the far wall. Office furniture and equipment were stacked in a far corner, and Jen walked that way.

Grant yelled and several shelves tipped over. Jen shined her flashlight that way. "You guys all right?"

Grunts, crashes, and scuffing feet came from their direction. Jen holstered her pistol and drew her axe, then stepped toward the noise.

Something grabbed her free arm and yanked her back.

14

The hand let go as Jen spun and swung the axe. Damn thing sliced through air, the action knocking her off balance and onto the floor.

"Wait," a voice above her screamed. "We're human. Don't hurt us."

Jen turned her flashlight toward the voice, illuminating a woman in a dirty business skirt and jacket, her eyes wild.

Zeke's voice called out. "I've got one."

Jen glanced to where another beam glowed by the shelves.

Mark appeared next to the woman. He had his mace in hand. "Who are you and why did you attack?"

The girl shivered and wrapped her arms around herself. "I'm Sharon Watson. I used to work here. Pridger's Accounting on the fifth floor." Her voice squeaked as she said, "Please don't hurt us."

Grant and Zeke arrived escorting a man in a shabby suit between them. Zeke had the man's arm locked behind his back. "And you?" Jen asked.

"John Dormand," he said. "Senior partner at Pridger's."

"Why'd you attack us?" Mark asked.

"I didn't," Dormand said. "I was hiding and this one"—he pointed at Grant—"tripped over me."

Mark swung his gaze to Sharon. "And you?"

"I-I didn't attack anyone," she said. "I heard you talking and knew you weren't one of the creatures. Then I saw your lights. I didn't want to startle you by speaking, so I touched your arm."

Jen lowered her axe. "Is it just you two, or is anyone else gonna jump out at us?"

"Just us," Dormand said. "We've been down here for weeks." He added, "I think."

"You think?" Grant asked.

Dormand shrugged. "At first, there were four of us and we'd go upstairs and scavenge the building. But it became more dangerous. We lost the other two. Sharon and I decided to stay here until we ran out of food. We haven't seen the sun since."

Another explosion rocked the building. A large crash came from up the stairway.

"What's going on out there?" Sharon asked.

"The army's bombing us," Grant said.

Jen wiped dust from her eyes. "We need to get to the sewer system. Do you know where the entrance is?"

"Will you bring us with you?" Sharon asked.

"Of course." Mark's voice softened. "Where's the sewer entrance?"

Sharon pointed to a pile of desks. "I'm pretty sure it's underneath them. They've been there for months, but I noticed a manhole cover in the floor before they were stacked there."

Jen ran to the desks and pulled one off the top. It bounced on the floor, breaking a leg off in the process.

Grant and Zeke joined in. Jen handed her flashlight to Sharon. "Can you hold that for us?"

Sharon nodded and lit the desk pile.

Jen and Mark worked together to pull desks off the pile and out of the way.

Another strike on the building caused the pile of desks to fall over. Jen smiled. "Butler doesn't know he's helping us now."

In minutes they uncovered a four-foot-wide manhole.

Grant stuck two fingers in the manhole cover's notch and pulled. His face squinched and arms strained, but the damn thing didn't move. He straightened, puffing. "Weighs a ton."

"We need a lever," Mark said. "Crowbar or something like it."

"I found a metal bar when we first came down here," Dormand said. "Was going to use it as a weapon in case any of those things got down here, but it was too heavy."

Mark tossed him a flashlight. "Show us."

The building shook and something heavy slammed the floor above them, causing Jen to duck. "Shit. I thought it was coming through."

Dormand led Mark to the stairs and pointed the beam to the side. "There."

Mark picked up and returned with a four-foot piece of rebar.

Another strike and the floor above collapsed at the stairs. Debris flew into the basement, followed by a cloud of dust. Jen coughed. "We're out of time."

Mark stuck the rebar in the notch and rubbed his hands

together. He grasped the end and pushed down. The cover didn't move. Jen grabbed the bar in front of Mark, and Zeke and Grant ahead of her.

Dust made it difficult to see the cover. Grant sounded like he was coughing up a lung.

"Get those lights closer to the manhole," Jen yelled.

Seconds later, she could just make out the cover.

"On three," Mark yelled. "Give it all you've got. If we get it up, roll it to the right." He choked and went into a coughing fit.

Another crash. This one close. *The damn thing's about to come down on our heads.*

"One, two, three!"

Jen pushed down, grunting. It moved, but barely. The bar rose as the others released it.

The ceiling collapsed not more than ten feet from her. A piece of solid debris struck her foot. *Damn, that hurts.*

"This is it," she yelled. "Give it more than you've got."

Two more sets of hands joined them. "One, two, three," Mark yelled.

The bar dipped lower and the cover teetered on the other end. "Roll it to the right," Mark gasped.

Sweat poured down Jen's face and her arm muscles trembled. Teeth gritted, she strained to keep the cover up. It moved, but how much she couldn't tell. Someone let go and the bar rose. Then someone else let go and the weight and strain on Jen's arms were too much. She lost her sweaty grip and the cover slammed down.

Jen dropped to her knees. She grabbed one of the flashlights and pointed it at the manhole. The cover partially covered the opening, leaving a three-foot gap.

"We can get through," she yelled.

A dark figure swept past her and shined a light down the hole. "There are rungs," Zeke said. "I'll go first." He disappeared down the hole.

The building shivered under another strike. It was in its dying throes.

Jen grabbed Sharon's arm and led her to the manhole. "Hurry down."

Sharon nodded and climbed down out of sight. Dormand was next. He hesitated. "What if those things are down there?"

Jen pulled her pistol and pointed it at his face. "Down. Now!"

Dormand hurried down the rungs.

She coughed. *Can barely breathe in this shit.* "Mark, you and Grant next."

"What?" Mark said. "No way."

"No time to argue. We need you both down there in case there are zombies. Go."

Mark slid onto his stomach and disappeared over the edge. Grant followed.

The ceiling above Jen let out a deafening crack. Jen jumped into the hole as the ceiling caved in. Pieces of concrete struck her in the head and shoulder as she fell. She slammed into someone and knocked them off the rungs, both of them landing in ankle-deep water.

Someone grabbed her arms and pulled her away as a ton of concrete and plaster poured from the hole.

Jen was lifted to her feet and guided farther into the sewer. "This way," Zeke said. She stumbled alongside him, hacking. His flashlight barely penetrated the dust.

They reached a turn in the tunnel and the dust cleared. Mark stumbled in front of her, Grant's arm over his shoulder. Grant looked as bad as she felt. Sharon stood off to the side with her flashlight on the others.

Mark let Grant go and the soldier stood, bent over, with his hands on his knees, vomiting. Mark's eyes teared, leaving streaks in the dust on his face. Jen pushed off gently from Zeke. "I can stand." Zeke stepped back as she leaned against the wall. She wiped her face with her arm and gagged. "What the hell did I land in? I reek."

Grant straightened. "Thanks for falling and knocking me into that shit. And I mean it literally. I think I swallowed a turd."

"Wait," Mark said. "Where's Dormand?"

"He went the other way. Said he knew a safe place in that direction." Sharon put her head in her hands and sobbed.

"What's our next step?" Grant asked.

Mark examined at Jen. "Your head's bleeding pretty good." He cut off one of his sleeves and pressed it to her forehead. "Hold this."

Jen held the cloth to her forehead and Mark pulled the ends of the sleeve behind her head and tied it. "You'll be OK. Scalp wounds look worse than they are."

He turned to the others. "I say we try to find an exit to the street and see where we are."

Grant nodded. "Good idea. Figure out what direction we need to go. We could be moving farther away from the base for all we know."

"We should at least find some shelter before night comes," Jen said.

Zeke brushed himself off. Covered in dust, his ninja uniform made him look more like a ghost than an assassin. He shined his flashlight down the sewer tunnel. "Follow me."

Twenty minutes later, the air became more breathable and the sounds of destruction faded into the distance.

"There." Grant pointed to a smaller manhole. Thin beams of light broke through the cover's holes.

Mark moved beneath it and put his foot on a rung. "I'll check it out. Stay here and I'll let you know if it's clear."

He climbed, the heels of his boots making each rung give off a muffled *ring*.

When he reached the cover, he pressed his shoulder against it. It lifted and sunlight hit his face, causing him to squint.

Sliding the cover out of his way, he stuck his head out of the manhole and looked around. Seconds later, he ducked his head inside. "All clear up here. Everybody up." He pulled himself up.

After everyone got out, Jen helped Grant slide the cover back into place. Zeke had his katana out and gave it a few practice swings. "How about I go scout?"

"I think we're better off sticking together." Mark had his mace in his hand. "Only close-combat weapons. No firearms."

Jen's watch showed ten minutes to noon. *Can't tell direction from the sun yet.* "Need to get our bearings. Follow me."

"How are we going to tell where we are?" Grant asked. "We don't know this city."

"I do." Sharon stepped forward.

Jen led the way to the alley entrance and peered out into the street. No sign of zombies. *And no artillery.* She waved Sharon forward and pointed to a street sign. "Second Street. What direction is the base?"

Sharon pointed behind them and to the left. "Interstate 90 is a couple of blocks behind us. If we follow it west to Highway 2, it'll take us to the base."

"Sounds like a plan," Mark said. "Let's head toward the interstate and grab a vehicle on the way."

Jen jogged to the other end of the alley and popped her head out just as a dozen zombies rushed by in a V formation. The leader, an unusually tall shirtless man with coarse autopsy stitches across his chest, whirled around and rushed at her with the rest on his heels.

15

J en backpedaled into the alley. "Horde coming!"

A hand pressed on her back. "We're with you." Mark stepped next to her.

The zombies rushed into the alley, the leader nowhere in sight. *Where the hell is he?*

Jen reared her arm back, grasping the axe tight enough to turn her knuckles white. She timed her overhead swing and brought the blade down on the first zombie's head. A man in mechanic's overalls with the name Brad stitched over the pocket, he dropped at her feet.

Mark's mace was a blur as he bashed first one zombie, then another. One of them fell and the other staggered. Mark gave the second one another lick and it went down.

Zeke jumped past them, his katana blade slashing. "Leave some for me and Betty."

He spun and took out the next three in seconds.

Still the horde pushed forward. The narrowness of the alley prevented more than three from attacking at once.

Grant tapped Jen on the shoulder. "Fall back. I'll take a few."

Jen dropped back and Grant drove the tip of his sword under a fat zombie's jaw and into his brain. The zombie fell before Grant could pull his blade out, and the tall man took the sword down with him.

Jen grabbed Grant's collar and yanked him back just as an old woman sprung at him. Jen followed through with her axe and hit the zombie in the shoulder, knocking it over.

She stepped forward, split the skull of the next zombie in line, then planted the blade in the old woman's forehead.

Only three zombies left. Jen zeroed in on the leader, who stood back from the others and watched the battle.

Jen shoved past the other two undead and bulled her way to him. At the last second, he ducked and Jen's axe sailed over his head. She lost her balance, slammed against the wall, and fell to the ground. Her axe flew out of her grasp. The leader stood over her, his yellow eyes sizing her up.

Zeke finished off the last of the attackers and sprang for the leader, who sidestepped him and dashed out of the alley.

"Zeke," Mark yelled. "Hold up."

Zeke stopped at the end of the alley. "I can catch him."

Jen sat up and Grant helped her to her feet. "That was a leader," she said. "He'll probably take you right to another horde."

"And will probably bring them back here," Mark said.

Jen turned to see how Sharon was, but she'd disappeared. "Sharon?"

Grant looked back. "Shit." He ran to the other end of the alley and peered up and down the street. Walking back to Jen, he shook his head. "No sign of her."

"Must've gotten scared and took off," Mark said.

"We've got to go find her," Grant said.

"Can't," Jen said. "No time. We got lucky this was a small horde and they stacked up in the alley. We won't get that lucky a second time."

Mark sighed. "We did what we could. She survived long enough for us to find her. She might find a place to lay low and wait things out."

Jen patted Grant on the back. "Come on."

Grant nodded and they walked out onto the deserted street.

"She said the highway's a couple of blocks this way," Jen said. "Let's find a vehicle."

Cars were parked every which way along the street, with some crowding the middle. Jen opened the door of a large SUV and checked for keys. None.

An engine started and a minivan pulled out from the curb. Zeke stuck his head out of the driver's window. "Got one. Almost a full tank, too. Come on."

Jen raced to the van and slid the side door open. "You know how to drive?"

"Hell, yeah," Zeke said. He gunned the engine.

"I'm not talking about driving in a freaking computer game," Jen said.

Grant ran up. "Maybe I should drive. That's what I do."

Dashing over from the other side of the road, Mark yelled, "Get in. They're coming."

Sure enough, a huge horde zeroed in on them from two blocks away. They filled the whole damn street.

Jen jumped into the back and slid over. Grant took the passenger seat next to Zeke.

Mark dived in. "Go!"

Zeke hit the accelerator and left tire marks and black smoke in his wake.

Mark slammed the door closed and sat up. He glanced over his shoulder. "Keep going. We need to lose them."

Jen sat forward and pointed to the next street. "Take a right there."

The tires screeched as Zeke threw the van into a tight turn. It sideswiped a police car, tearing off its side-view mirror.

Zeke laughed. "Couldn't have gotten away with that a month ago."

Jen glanced behind them. The horde hadn't stopped, but had fallen back. "Take it easy, Zeke. We're outdistancing them, but if you get us in an accident, we're toast."

"There." Grant pointed at the interstate on-ramp.

Zeke took the van into the turn without Jen's heart jumping into her throat, and they entered the interstate. Abandoned vehicles littered the highway, and Zeke did a great job avoiding them and keeping speed. Jen watched the rear, but saw no sign of the horde.

Two miles farther, Grant pointed ahead. "Look at that. It's the cavalry."

A convoy of five Humvees headed their way. Mark tapped Zeke on the shoulder. "Pull over."

Zeke slowed the van and stopped. Mark and Jen got out and waved their arms. A gunner on the lead Humvee waved back, and the Humvees pulled up several yards in front of them.

The lead gunner yelled, "Who are you?"

Grant got out. "I'm assigned to Supply. These people are a scientific team studying the zombies. They report to Colonel Butler."

The lead vehicle's driver's door opened and a sergeant stepped out. "Load up. One of you in each vehicle. I'll radio in and let them know we're coming."

Jen took the lead vehicle. The sergeant put the radio mic to his lips. "Echo Eight to Control. We've picked up one of our Supply Specialists and three civilians. Please inform Control One."

"Echo Eight, this is Control One. Bring them to my location immediately."

"Roger, Control One. En route."

The Humvee made a U turn and the convoy sped back to the base.

Sergeant Howell met them at the Headquarters building. "The colonel wants to see you right away."

Jen scowled. "I'd like to see him, too."

Howell led them into the building and to Butler's office door. He knocked.

"Enter," Butler said.

Howell opened the door and waved the group in. He closed the door, staying out in the hall.

Butler's desk stood in the corner. Made of an expensive-looking dark wood, the damn thing shined. *Probably has some poor private first class wax it every day.* The rest of the office was spartan, with a second door next to the desk, but not much else.

Mark stood with his fists clenched, while Grant stood at attention. Zeke studied the ceiling tiles.

Butler leaned back in his leather chair, with the American and Army flags flanking him. "I'm glad to see you've made it back in one piece. When are you leaving?"

Jen clenched her jaw. *What an asshole.* "Why? Don't want another chance to kill us?"

Butler's face turned bright crimson in an instant. "How dare you accuse me."

Mark bent forward with his fists on Butler's desk. "It wouldn't be the first time. How about Major Morris and his men in Afghanistan? Same thing, except this time you didn't just leave us, you tried to bomb the shit out of us."

Butler rose, his voice trembling. "I want you out of here now. All of you." He pointed at Grant. "Get back to your damn unit."

He turned to Jen. "And you're the worst of the bunch. I've half a mind to place you into custody."

Time to play the trump card. "What do you think Dr. Cartwright would have to say about that?"

Butler's lips pressed together and he said nothing.

Jen propped her hands on her hips. *Let's make this even better.* "Fuck you, Butler. We're going to finish our mission and you're going to support us. Screw with us again, and I'll recommend to Dr. Cartwright that you're removed from your position." She had no idea if Cartwright would support her on that, but neither did he.

Butler's eyes narrowed and he clenched his fists. "I will follow my orders." He pointed a finger at Jen. "But any of you step out of line and I'll lock your asses up and ship you out."

Jen patted Zeke on the shoulder. "I'm hungry. Anyone ready for lunch?" She glanced at Butler as she left the room. His face was turning color again.

16

J en scooped a mouthful of mashed potatoes into her mouth. Zeke and Mark had been silent since they left Butler's office, only offering comments about the food selection in the chow hall.

Grant separated himself as soon as they walked in and sat with some soldiers on the other side of the hall.

Jen swallowed and took a sip of water. "I have an idea for next steps."

Mark wiped his mouth with a paper napkin. "If it's got something to do with taking Butler down, then I'm in."

Zeke picked up the top of his hamburger bun and examined the contents. "Two pickles? Cheap bastards."

"Zeke," Jen said. "Focus. Eat the damn burger as it is and listen up."

Zeke sighed and placed the top of the bun back in place. "I think we should go kill more zombies. Find their leaders and take them out."

Mark's eyebrow rose. "Not a bad tactical idea."

Jen leaned forward. "I need to talk to Cartwright first. Give her a full report."

"And then?" Mark asked.

"Butler's hiding something. Otherwise, why try to kill us? He doesn't want us around, and we won't leave."

Zeke took a bite of his hamburger. "So what's he hiding?" Pieces of chewed food fell onto his plate.

Jen made a face at him. "Don't ninjas have some sort of reputation for being neat and orderly?"

Zeke shook his head.

"Anyway," Jen said, "I don't know what he's up to, but it's pretty obvious it has to do with Area 51."

Mark shrugged. "Agreed. So what—" His face slackened. "You want to break into a guarded, probably alarmed, restricted area on a military base."

Jen grinned. "Glad we're on the same track."

"Look, Jen," Mark said. "I'm all for taking Butler down, but I want to get to my family."

"I'm in," Zeke said.

Jen stared at Mark. "I promised you I'd go with you to make sure your family's OK, and I plan on keeping that promise. But I'd feel a lot better if you joined me on this. I wouldn't have gotten out of Anchorage without you." She patted his arm. "You're like my good luck charm."

Mark squeezed his eyes shut and sighed. "You've saved me, too. But keeping up with you is a pain in the ass."

"This is the asshole that let soldiers die in Afghanistan and left us out to dry in Anchorage. I think the sky's the limit for his next backstab. Don't you?"

Mark opened his eyes. "Yeah, I'll do it. But on one condition."

"What's that?"

"You tell Cartwright what you're planning. If she tells you not to do it, then we don't."

No idea what Cartwright will say. "It's a deal."

Thirty minutes later, Jen stood in front of the conference room monitor, the screen filled with Cartwright sitting at her desk.

"Your observations about the leader zombies is intriguing," Cartwright said. "It leads me to believe the virus does something to the live human brain that it doesn't get a chance to do to a bitten victim before he dies. This adds a worrisome dimension to the situation. We'll begin experiments on that theory immediately."

She leaned forward. "I also agree with your assessment of Colonel Butler. He's shown signs of instability and the military hierarchy is concerned. My apprehension is that he'll try to kill you again. And if he really is unstable, he may not care if I find out. I think my influence with him is hanging by a thread."

"Do you think we should just cut our losses and get out of here?" Mark asked.

Jen shot him a glare.

Cartwright put a finger to the corner of her mouth and looked off camera. "It's a risk I don't want you to take." She peered over her glasses at the screen. "Tell me again about the restricted area."

"There's a guard at the front gate and another at the back gate that controls entry into the loading dock."

Cartwright waved her hand as if to shoo a fly. "No. The man. The civilian you saw. Describe him."

"Short, older guy," Jen said. "Big round glasses, what hair he still had is gray."

Typing sounds came from the speakers. "Just a minute," Cartwright said, turning her back to the monitor.

"Was this the man?" she asked, facing them again. She held up a sheet of paper with the picture of the civilian they'd seen.

"That's him," Jen said.

Cartwright looked at the monitor and lowered her voice. "Who's in the room with you?"

"Just me, Mark, and Zeke."

"His name is Dr. Jeffrey Morgan. He was once a respected research neurologist."

"Once?" Mark asked.

"Yes. Once, but no more. Not after being arrested for experimenting on humans."

"Shit," Jen said. "What kind of experiments?"

"Mind control, implanting memories, that kind of thing." Cartwright straightened. "I had information he was there, but not what he was up to."

"Information?" Mark said. "From who?"

"Another time," Cartwright said. "Just understand that whatever Dr. Morgan's working on is guaranteed to be a threat."

"How did he end up here?" Jen asked.

Cartwright adjusted her glasses. "Exactly what I'd like to know. He disappeared while out on bail awaiting trial, and there's been no trace of him until now."

Zeke cleared his throat. "Sounds like we need a ninja infiltration of Area 51 to see what's going on in there."

Jen jerked a thumb at Zeke. "Kung Fu Panda here is right. Someone has to see what's going on."

Cartwright sighed. "I have an asset on base who reports only to me, and has been in Area 51. There's a top floor that's heavily secured that Morgan disappears into. My asset doesn't have access to that floor."

"Who's the asset?" Jen asked.

Cartwright ignored her question and peered over her glasses. "And there's another issue. I need you back here to get more of your blood."

"You didn't get enough the first time?"

"We're running out of what Doc sent, and you're the only survivor of Point Wallace."

Mark cleared his throat. "What difference does that make? Pretty much everyone has been infected."

Cartwright steepled her fingers. "Jen received a higher concentration than anyone else, and I need to see if it affects her differently over time." She sat back. "It could lead to a dead end, or a significant breakthrough. I can't tell at this point, but I'm leaving no stone unturned."

"So we break into the top floor of Area 51, find out what's going on, and get Jen down to you," Zeke said. "Sounds simple enough to me."

"No," Cartwright said. "My asset can pursue Butler's plans. I need Jen here."

Mark sighed. "As much as I want to get out of here, your plan doesn't make sense, Doctor. Unless your asset is willing to blow his or her cover, we're the best shot you have of finding out what the hell's going on here."

Jen crossed her arms and stared at the floor. If they just left, who knows what Butler could pull? He'd already shown many times over that he'd sacrifice others for what he wanted. *Besides, it's not guaranteed that studying my blood will actually help stop the zombies.*

She looked up. "I think I can do both. A quick try to see what Butler's got up his sleeve, and then we leave. I'm tired of just reacting to shit. Time to go on the offensive."

"That would be unadvisable." Cartwright removed her glasses and rubbed her eyes. "But also valuable."

Jen patted Zeke on the back. "Looks like we're in the spy business."

"We?" Zeke said.

Jen grinned. "You don't think I'm letting you have all the fun yourself, do you?"

Mark sighed.

"Jen." Cartwright's face softened. "I won't give you orders; Doc made it clear to me that doing so would create the opposite effect. But as someone who cares about what happens to you, I urge you to reconsider. There's little I can do to help you from here."

Jen wavered. *Not fair. She brought up Doc. My biggest failure.* She jutted her jaw forward. "I'm going to do this for Doc. And everyone else."

Cartwright leaned forward and the monitor went black.

"Are you nuts?" Mark asked. "You've done some crazy shit, but this is in another ballpark. A restricted area with armed guards and an insane commander?"

Jen smiled, but inwardly cringed. She'd gotten caught up in the moment, and Mark was bringing her back to earth. "We need to get out of this room before we get caught. Zeke, check the hallway."

Zeke opened the door. "All clear."

Jen strode into the hallway and to her room. Mark and Zeke joined her.

"All right," Mark said. "What's the plan? How are you going to infiltrate Area 51?"

"I can sneak in there at night," Zeke said. "I blend in with the shadows."

Jen waved him off. "There's a better way. Who do we know with access to the loading dock?"

"Grant?" Mark said.

Jen shrugged. "Every day at three a.m. And there are some quiet buildings along his route where no one would notice him stopping for a minute and taking on an extra load."

"And that would be you," Mark said.

Jen grinned. "Exactly. Zeke, think you can get another note to Grant?"

"Easy," Zeke said. "But do you think Grant will go along with it?"

"I don't know," she said. "But either way I'm getting into Area 51 to find out what the hell Butler's trying to hide."

17

K neeling behind some old barrels on the side of the rec center, Jen shivered in the early morning darkness.

"I still think I should go with you," Mark said, his voice startling her.

"It'll be easier to sneak around if it's just me."

"At least bring me along," Zeke said. "Sneaking is what I do."

Jen nudged him. "You would be the person they'd expect to try something like this. Besides, I need both of you out here in case I run into trouble."

A truck rumbled in the near distance. Jen's pulse picked up. The truck drew closer. *Will Grant risk himself to help out?*

The sigh of hydraulics and the squeak of brakes signaled it had stopped out front. A door opened and closed.

Jen gave Mark and Zeke a thumbs-up and dashed around the side of the building. The truck blocked her from the road and the back of it faced her. *Good job, Grant.*

She pulled the door up and rolled into the back, pulling the handle down behind her.

She turned on her flashlight. Surrounded by crates and boxes, she stumbled as the truck started moving with a jerk.

Have to find somewhere to hide.

She squeezed between two pallets and ducked behind a third. She'd had an idea of jumping into a box and letting the soldiers carry her off, but all the damn boxes were secure and the crates nailed shut.

The truck slowed, then stopped. Voices came from outside. Grant's was one, but she couldn't make out the words. The truck moved forward, continued for a couple of minutes, then turned and backed up, the warning beeps loud enough for her to hear them clearly.

With the squeal of brakes, it stopped and the engine went silent. A door opened and closed. Seconds later, another truck started and pulled out, its engine noise dimming in the distance.

The door rolled up, spilling light into the back. Jen pushed back behind a pallet.

"What've we got today?" a deep voice asked.

A woman's voice answered, "Same old shit, I'll bet. Steak and wine for the colonel and his civilian, and canned spaghetti for us."

Deep Voice laughed. "Butler says we're the elite troops, but we get fed worse than the others going to the chow hall."

Someone jumped onto the back and a banging came from that direction. Jen peeked out. A burly soldier had jammed a crowbar beneath a crate's lid and was trying to pry it up.

"Gimme a hand, Jonesy," he said.

A buffed up female soldier with short black hair joined him. "One, two, three."

They pushed, and with a ripping sound, the crate lid rose on one side.

Jonesy reached a hand in. "Holy shit, if this is what I think it is..."

She pulled on something then removed her hand. It held a can of beer.

"Are you kidding?" Deep Voice said. "That must've been a mistake."

Jonesy popped the top and downed a swallow. "Mmmm."

Deep Voice pulled another can from the crate. "This damn thing is full of them."

Jonesy swallowed and smacked her lips. "Are you thinking what I'm thinking?"

Deep Voice tilted his head. "No. What?"

She swatted him on the shoulder. "Sometimes I wonder just how dumb you can get."

He shrugged.

"If this crate goes to the food stores, the supply clowns will drink it all."

"So what do we do?" Deep Voice asked.

Jonesy rolled her eyes. "We grab a case for ourselves and go rat-hole it right now."

Deep Voice smiled. "Good idea." He reached in and hauled out a case.

Jonesy grabbed another one. "One for you and one for me." She slapped Deep Voice's hand as he went to get a third. "No more," she said. "They won't report a couple missing, but might if we take too many."

The back of the truck shuddered. Jen peeked out. Deep Voice and Jonesy stood on the dock. Deep Voice picked up both cases and put one on each shoulder. "You stay here and I'll go hide them."

"Like hell," Jonesy said. "I'm going with you. I want to know where mine is."

"But what if someone comes by and sees us gone?"

Jonesy strode to a door, punched numbers in a keypad, and held it open. "Then we better be quick about it."

I need to get through that door.

Deep Voice stepped through and Jonesy followed him, releasing the door.

Jen dashed out of the truck and to the door. She reached out as it closed and caught the handle before the door clicked shut. She puffed her cheeks and let out a breath. *Close.*

Sticking her head into the hallway, she looked right, peering down a long corridor that ended in a door with a meshed window. Jonesy had just walked through the doorway.

Down the other direction, two doors stood on the right side of the hallway. No sign of anyone there.

Those doors probably lead to the front of the building. Not what I'm looking for.

She stepped into the hallway, eased the door closed with a click, and padded to the meshed doorway, where she peeked through the window at a stairway. Voices came from above and were getting closer. She slipped beneath the bottom stairs and held her breath while footsteps scuffed above her.

The door to the hallway opened and Jonesy said, "See. Told you it'd only take a minute."

After the door closed Jen crept to the window. Deep Voice and Jonesy disappeared through the doorway to the loading dock.

Stepping softly, Jen climbed the first flight of stairs and then the second, where a door marked with the number two stood at the landing.

She peeked through the mesh window and ducked back down. Soldiers walked up and down the hall, some with papers in their hands and others fully armed.

She climbed to the third floor. Fewer soldiers there, but still too risky to try. *Dammit.*

The fourth floor had multiple doors along the hallway on either side, but no soldiers in sight. Jen grasped the door handle and turned it. A soldier walked out of an office that stood five feet in front of her, and headed the opposite way down the hall.

Jen released the handle and ducked. Pulse pounding in her ears, she peeked through the window. The soldier disappeared out the door at the other end of the hall. She got a flash of another stairway before the door closed.

Clasping her hand to her chest, she willed her heart to slow down. She looked down to see she'd gripped her axe's handle involuntarily.

She snuck up the stairs to the fifth floor, where a metal door with no windows greeted her. A keypad lay on the wall to the side.

This would be the place that Cartwright's asset couldn't penetrate. Definitely something going on in there.

"Looks like it's door number four," she said.

Jen crept down the stairs to the fourth floor. She watched through the window for a minute and detected no one. Voices came from below her on the stairs.

Shit.

Cracking the door open, she slipped inside the hallway.

The top of a head appeared down the stairs. Mouth dry, she ducked and hurried to the first office but the knob wouldn't turn. *Dammit.*

She rushed to the next door across the hall, and it, too, was locked. Voices from the stairs grew louder, and Jen's mouth went dry. The third door open easily and she ducked into the darkened room, closing the door behind her with a clunk that sounded like a gunshot. Her breath came in shallow gasps as she waited in the dark.

The voices approached and stopped in front of the door. A drop of sweat ran down her cheek. *Don't come in here. Don't come in here.*

"Colonel Butler wants that report by the end of the day," a man's voice with the hint of a Boston accent said.

Another voice grunted and a door across the hall squeaked. "Yeah, yeah. I know the drill."

The door closed and one set of footsteps echoed down the hall. Another door opened and closed, and then there was silence.

Jen fumbled along the wall and flipped a switch. The sudden light blinded her and she squinted.

When her eyes adjusted, she took inventory of the room. Shelves laden with cleaning supplies lined one wall. A mop and bucket stood next to a sink, and several sizes of brooms lay stacked in a corner.

Her mind searched for a way to the fifth floor. A pair of janitor overalls hung from a hook. *I could dress as a janitor and fake my way in.*

She scoffed. *Stupid. How would I get past a keypad?*

A clock on the wall showed she'd already been inside for almost twenty minutes. Mark and Zeke would be wondering what she'd found.

Maybe I should just find a way out and get to Atlanta.

Rubbing her shoulder, she tipped her head back to stretch her neck muscles and her attention settled on a large ventilation grate on the wall.

Bingo.

18

T he step stool squeaked and tilted to one side as Jen balanced herself on the top step. She caught her breath and put a hand against the wall to steady herself.

Don't tell me after all this I'm going to get taken out by a shitty piece of janitorial equipment.

She pulled the screwdriver she'd found in a toolbox from her pocket and removed the four screws holding the cover on. Holding the screwdriver between her teeth, she used both hands to pry the cover off the wall. A dusty breeze hit her in the face and she turned her head to sneeze.

Her flashlight beam showed dust bunnies as big as rats in the shaft. *Great thought, Jen. Thanks.*

The shaft went left and right. To the left there were other openings farther down until the light could reach no more. To the right, it went several feet until it met a vertical shaft.

Jen laid the flashlight in the vent and tried to jiggle the vent. Three feet by three feet, it was made of thick metal and didn't move.

Satisfied, she clicked the flashlight off, stuck it in her belt, and climbed down the ladder.

A door opened and closed nearby. Jen readied her axe and stood to the side of the door. Footsteps clicked on the tile past her door. Another door opened and closed, and there was silence.

She considered locking the door, but it might draw suspicion. She had to find a way to avoid alarm while she was in the vent. Her eyes roved over the contents of the room and settled on a plastic placard leaning against the mop bucket. It said "Caution Wet Floor." She smiled.

Two minutes later, she'd taped a piece of paper underneath the vent opening that said "Vent Repairs in Progress by Order of Colonel Butler." Butler had the soldiers so cowed they wouldn't dare to question him on it.

She secured her axe on her back. If she was going to be sliding around on her stomach, she didn't want that thing scratching the vent and bringing unwanted attention. She climbed the ladder and pulled herself into the vent, sliding to the right. Once she was fully in, she took out her flashlight and shined it toward the vertical shaft.

It only took a minute to reach it. She pointed the beam down and saw where it split off into the next two floors below her.

She rolled onto her back to look up and regretted it when the axe dug into her back. Shit. *No good place for that thing.*

Gritting her teeth, she pointed the light upward. The opening for the next floor lay twelve feet away.

Jen slid her upper body into the shaft and grabbed onto a two-inch outcropping where two sections of vents were fastened together. *Not going to be easy.*

She pulled her upper body up while sliding her lower

extremities farther out. Her fingers burned with the effort. Worse still, they became slick with sweat. Raising herself again, she grasped the next outcropping with one hand, then repeated the process.

Only her feet remained in the horizontal vent. She strained to pull them out. They slid slowly and stopped. Her breath came in short gasps.

One, two, three. Pull.

Her feet slipped out and banged the side of the shaft. Jen's slick fingers lost their grip and she fell, feet first down the shaft, her hands desperately clutching for something, anything to hold on to.

She spread her legs, her feet hit an outcropping, and she stopped with a bang that echoed through the vents. She thrust her arms up and grabbed an outcropping above her.

Jen's head drooped forward and sweat ran down her face. *Too close to quit. Come on, finish this shit.*

She wiped first one hand, then the other on her shirt, then reached for the next outcropping. Moving slowly, but methodically, she climbed her way back up to the horizontal vent she'd come from. She stopped and listened, but there was no shouting, no signs of pursuit.

Gulping air, she continued upward, arriving at the fifth-floor vent a few minutes later. She pulled herself inside and collapsed, her heart racing and muscles burning.

On her elbows and knees, she inched toward the first vent opening and stopped at the grate. Bile spilled into the back of her throat. *The smell. The graveyard smell.*

It was dark as pitch, but Jen sensed something moving just beneath the vent, and she leaned back from the grate. *They're keeping zombies up here? For what?*

Another movement came from across the room, along with the clinking of chains.

Jen crawled to the next vent opening and the death smell faded. Unlike the previous room, this one—an office with a cluttered desk—was well lit. A computer on the desk was on and had a document displayed, but Jen couldn't read it from her position. Several stocked bookshelves ran along one wall.

Voices came from farther down the vent. She crawled closer to it and froze when Butler said, "You better have made progress."

She slid up to the vent opening. The room was a cross between a lab and a surgery. Computers, beakers, and other instruments lined counters against the walls, while an operating table stood in the middle of the room. Strapped to that table lay a soldier, the top of his skull removed and wires running to some type of probes inserted into his brain. His eyes were open, but he showed no signs of life.

Jen squinted to get a good look. Yellow eyes.

The wires ran to a machine on the counter, and Morgan stood next to it, adjusting a slider.

Butler towered next to him, his hands on his hips. "We're out of time, Doctor. My superiors are asking too many questions."

Dr. Morgan didn't reply and continued working the controls.

Butler's face reddened. "Doctor," he yelled.

Morgan looked up at Butler and blinked as if coming out of a dream. "What is it, Colonel?"

Butler clenched his fists, but answered calmly. "I need to know when you expect a successful test."

Morgan removed his small, round wire-framed glasses and blew on them before replacing them. "Science doesn't run on timelines, Colonel." Butler scowled, and Morgan raised a hand. "But in this case, I've made some headway.

"As you recall, my plan was to control the undead electronically. Watch Corporal Stennings there on the table."

Holy shit. Dr. Frankenstein stuff.

Morgan turned a dial. The zombie soldier didn't move. Butler grunted and his jaw clenched.

Morgan adjusted a slider, then said, "I think we have it now." He turned the dial again.

The zombie kicked a leg out.

Butler grinned. "What else can he do?"

Morgan stretched his back. "That's it so far."

Butler's eyebrows rose. "Are you fucking kidding? You made a dead man's leg move? I did that with a frog in high school."

Morgan frowned. "Of course, the results of electronic control hasn't been what I'd hoped."

"So what's Plan B?"

Morgan put a finger up. "I've found a way for you to start controlling the zombies today. Soon, you'll have your own army and no one will be able to stop you from marching on Washington."

19

J en squinted. *Butler controlling zombies? His own army? Against Washington? This shit can't be real.*

Morgan adjusted his glasses. "Do you remember the recording you provided me of the conversation between Dr. Cartwright and those refugees from Anchorage?"

Jen clenched her fists. *They taped us?*

Butler nodded. "Wish I'd started tapping their conversations sooner. So far, we only have their call from yesterday, and even then, only the first twenty minutes. My comm folks are new at that, but have assured me the tap won't drop again."

"I gleaned some interesting information from them," Morgan said. "A case in point is what they called leader zombies. These are humans that die without being bitten first. When they're reanimated they have the ability to communicate with, and control, zombies who were created from being bitten, which are called drones."

"Nice science lesson," Butler said. "What does that mean to me?"

Morgan stepped past Butler and pulled back a drape at the end of the room. Behind a large window, three zombies were chained to the wall. They strained uselessly to attack Morgan, their yellow eyes gleaming.

"Another demonstration," Morgan said. "I trust you recognize the zombie in the middle."

The zombie he pointed to wore military BDUs with several bullet holes in the chest. Jen couldn't make out his name tape because of a bloodstain.

Butler sauntered over to the window. "Captain Beal. You're looking a little worn." He chuckled at his own joke.

"Observe." Morgan pointed at Beal's head, where a bulky plastic helmet was strapped.

Morgan picked up a microphone and turned it on. "Captain Beal."

Beal went apeshit, flinging himself against his chains.

"Captain Beal," Morgan repeated. "Sit on the floor."

The zombie captain continued to flail against his restraints.

Morgan took a small device from his pocket. Black, with a red button, it fit snugly in his hand. He pressed the button.

Captain Beal's back arched and his arms flung out, fingers splayed. A mournful moan came from deep in his chest.

Morgan released the button, and Beal came out of his convulsions. Morgan spoke into the mic. "Captain Beal. Sit on the floor."

Chains rattling, the zombie captain lowered himself to the floor.

No freaking way.

The other two zombies, both with various chunks of flesh missing from their bodies, continued to lunge at the windows.

Butler clapped Morgan on the shoulder. "Now you're talking. Screw the fancy wires and shit. Discipline has always worked for me." He frowned. "How many of those helmets do you have and how do we control them from a distance? We'd need a couple million of them."

Morgan's face broke into a Cheshire grin. "We only have the one helmet at this time, but more can be manufactured within the week."

"One?" Butler yelled. "How many can we have within a week?"

"Thirty to fifty."

"What the fuck, Morgan? How the hell does that help me now?"

Morgan pushed his glasses up. "These helmets are fairly complex. It has a speaker, GPS tracker, and the circuitry to send a powerful localized EMP pulse into the zombie's brain."

Butler stepped nose-to-nose with Morgan. "I don't want a fucking science lesson. I want results, and I want them now."

Morgan calmly stared back at Butler. "If you'll step aside, I'll demonstrate."

Butler backed away, his face a bright crimson.

I've got a feeling I'm not going to like this.

"As I reported," Morgan said, "the EMP signal is what causes the zombie to feel pain. In fact, it's the only thing I've found that will do so. And the beauty of it is that it has to be powerful and concentrated, so the Pentagon can't just set up a huge EMP pulse to stop your army."

"Results, Doctor. Now."

Morgan sighed. "Observe. Remember, Captain Beal is a leader." He spoke into the microphone. "Captain Beal, tell your two zombie friends to sit."

Beal sat still, his yellow eyes searching the floor in front of him.

Morgan held up the torture device. "Captain Beal, do as I ask or I'll use this again."

Beal's gaze rose and focused on Morgan. Jen swallowed. That wasn't just a look of hunger. Beal's eyes held raw, pure hate.

As if on cue, the zombies on either side of Beal sat and became still.

"Holy shit," Butler yelled. "Just like that. Morgan, you're a genius."

Morgan beamed. "Control the leaders and you control them all."

"When can we get the other leaders fitted for their helmets?" Butler asked.

"My recommendation is to have as few leaders as possible." Morgan pulled the drapes back over the windows. "By reviewing drone footage, my preliminary analysis is that the average leader can control up to ten thousand drones. I recommend two hundred leaders. As I said earlier, we have the one helmet now and could have thirty to fifty more by next week."

Butler closed his eyes for a minute. "That's a half million loyal troops by next week." He slapped the doctor on the shoulder. "Now that's results." He frowned. "But I have to find forty-nine more leaders. And I want them with military experience."

"Why's that a problem?" Morgan asked.

Butler scowled. "Those are good men out there, some with families." Closing his eyes, he rubbed the bridge of his nose. "Maybe the cost of saving this country is too high."

Morgan removed his glasses. "Aren't you the one who will lead us to take back this country from the politicians?

To weed out and destroy the un-American influences in the halls of power?"

"Yes," Butler said. "I take no joy in the bloodshed that's to come. But once Washington falls, I believe we can get this great nation back to its roots. Back to its destiny." He straightened. "Then we'll move on to destroy our foreign enemies. Our undead army will be unstoppable."

This fucking guy is nuts. Enough observation bullshit. We've got to take him out.

Jen slid backward, past the office and the darkened room. *Where they probably have more poor saps chained up. Are they murdered soldiers, too?*

She shifted to her side and shined the flashlight behind her to the vertical shaft. *Another ten feet.*

Her axe slid on her back and she reached around to grab it, but missed. It hit the metal vent with a clatter, and Jen's heart stopped.

"What the hell was that?" Butler's voice came from ahead of her.

She stuck the axe in her belt and scurried backward, the damn thing banging with every move.

"Who's there?" Butler's head appeared through the vent opening. "Whoever you are, stop or you'll be shot."

Jen pressed on.

Butler's head disappeared, then reappeared with his arm. "I said stop." A muzzle flash illuminated him as an earsplitting bang rolled down the shaft. A bullet hit the side of the vent a foot in front of Jen.

Shit!

Doubling her efforts, Jen scrambled backward and her breath came in shallow pants. Seconds later, her feet dangled into the vertical shaft. Butler fired again and the round hit above Jen.

She lowered her feet until they hit an outcropping. She slid her upper body out of the vent just as Butler fired a third time. The bullet ricocheted off the vent an inch from her hand. She almost lost her grip on the vent, then disappeared down the shaft.

Not too fast. Don't slip.

She made it to the fourth-floor vent, crawled to the janitor's closet, and dropped to the floor.

A klaxon sounded, its blaring deafening. Shouting and footsteps came from the hallway.

Trapped.

20

T he damn alarm gave her a freaking headache. How to get out? Being aggressive had always worked for her before. *If it ain't broke, don't fix it.*

She found a blue ball cap and placed it on her head, pulled the brim down, and secured her axe to her back. Pulling down the overalls on the hook, she shook them out then threw them on.

Someone banged into the door, startling her. When the door remained closed, she picked up a broom with a wide brush and put her other hand on the doorknob. With a deep breath, she pulled the door open.

The alarm sounded ten times louder in the hall. Armed soldiers ran by shouting. She couldn't hear a damn thing they said. Backing into the room, she hesitated. It'd look more suspicious if anyone saw her trying to hide, so she stepped out into the hallway and ran to the stairway door. *Look like you belong here.*

A soldier had pushed the stairway door open and looked back at her. He held it and waved her through.

She ran down the steps to the next floor. When no one

stopped her, she kept going. Maybe she could get to the dock undetected and hide in the back of an empty truck. *Get out the same way I got in.*

She hit the first floor in a dead run and went to push the hallway door, when it opened and she stood face-to-face with Sergeant Howell.

They stared at each other for a moment, then he grabbed her arm. "Come with me."

Jen pulled her arm back and scrambled to pull her pistol, but the damn thing was under the overalls.

Howell let go and glanced over his shoulder. "We don't have time. If the wrong person sees you, you're screwed."

Jen flexed her arm. "And you're the right person?"

"I'm one that's not trying to kill you at the moment."

What the hell was she going to do? If he was telling the truth, he was her way out. If not, there wasn't much she could do to stop him.

What the hell. "I'll follow."

Howell strode down the hall. Jen kept pace.

Other soldiers, their rifles at the ready, ran by them and toward the stairs. Jen kept her head down and stayed behind Howell.

He took the door that led to the front of the building.

Passing empty offices on each side, they walked into the front lobby. *Still dark out.* Howell pulled back from the glass doors and stopped.

"Butler's standing out front," he said. "He's got two armed guards with him and he's watching everyone come out."

He peeked out and turned back to her. "Stay right behind me. I'll distract him and you keep on going."

"Why?" she asked. "Why are you doing this?"

He smiled. "We'll talk later. Get your friends and go to

the conference room. Don't call Dr. Cartwright. Wait for me."

Jen licked her lips. "OK."

"When I stop to talk to him, you keep going."

"Got it."

Howell followed several soldiers out the door, and Jen stayed in his shadow. Butler couldn't see her, but she couldn't see how close they were to him either.

Howell raised a hand. "Colonel, they think they have someone cornered on the fourth floor."

He stopped, and Jen walked around him and through the gate.

"Is there just the one?" Butler asked. "Do we know who it is?"

"No, sir."

"I'll bet it's those assholes working for Cartwright."

Jen wanted to run. Wanted to find Mark and Zeke. But she couldn't afford to bring any attention to herself.

She made a beeline toward the rec center. It stood dark and still. Slipping into the shadows, she put down the broom, leaned against the wall, placed her a hand on her knee, and barfed.

"Jen." A soft voice in her ear. She spun.

"Jen," Zeke repeated.

Jen reached out and pulled the skinny ninja into a hug. "I'm so glad to see you."

"You OK?" Mark's voice came from behind Zeke.

Jen chuckled. "I am now."

"What did you find out?" Zeke asked.

Butler. Howell had lured him off the scent, but it wouldn't be long before that shit head was looking for her.

"We're in deep shit. I need to talk to Cartwright. Now." She peeled off the overalls and hurried across the road.

Mark jogged to her side. "Did Butler see you? Is that why we have to hurry?"

Jen shook her head. "I'll tell you everything when we get to the conference room." She broke into a run.

They arrived at the conference room and entered. Zeke closed the door and Jen flipped the light switch.

Howell stood by the monitor, a pistol pointed at them. "Glad you could make it."

21

J en stepped toward Howell. He aimed the gun at her chest. "Not a good idea."

"Why the hell did you help me get out of Area 51 if you're doing this?" Jen asked.

"He helped you get out of there?" Mark leaned forward on the balls of his feet, his hands clenched into fists.

Howell swung the barrel towards him. "Why don't you all have a seat on that side of the table while I explain?"

Jen hesitated. If the three of them attacked at once, they might get him. But someone was sure to get hurt, or worse.

As if reading her thoughts, Howell said, "Please. Just hear me out. No need for anyone to get hurt."

Zeke took a seat and laid his scabbard on the table in front of him. *He's not fooling me. He could have that katana out and swinging in half a second.*

Jen pulled a chair out next to him and sat. Mark didn't move.

"I'll explain everything," Howell said. "We're on the same side."

Mark's jaw muscles clenched, but he sat next to Jen.

"As long as your hands stay on the table and you keep your seats, there's no need for this." Howell holstered his pistol. "My name is Lance Howell; however, I'm not who you think I am."

Jen smirked. "I'll bet you're really one of the Lost Boys. Or is it Tinkerbell?"

Howell grinned. "It'd take a lot more than that to get a rise out of me." He leaned over and set his hands on the tabletop. "I'm a CID Special Agent."

"CID?" Zeke said. "Are you a spy?"

"No." Howell straightened. "Army Criminal Investigation Division. More like an FBI Agent."

"So, Mr. Super Secret Agent," Jen said, "are you here because of us? Or because of Butler?"

Howell nodded. "I was told you're sharp as a tack, but with a bit of a mouth."

Jen frowned.

Howell held a hand up. "Let's not get off track. I'm here to investigate Colonel Butler and what's going on in Area 51."

"Cartwright said she had an asset here," Mark said. "How do we know it's you?"

Howell looked into Jen's eyes. "I'll eat a bug if I'm lying."

Jen glanced at Mark and Zeke. They looked back at her with raised eyebrows.

"Dr. Cartwright told me to tell you that," Howell said.

Jen leaned back in her seat and let out a loud breath. "I believe you."

Mark visibly relaxed. "I agree."

"And you?" Howell looked at Zeke.

"I'm cool if they are," Zeke said.

Howell nodded. "Let's call Dr. Cartwright and brief her. Then we need to get you to your plane."

Zeke pressed the console button on the conference

table. The monitor screen remained dark. "What's up with this?" Zeke pressed it again.

"Let me," Howell said. He pressed it. Nothing.

Zeke turned the controller over and checked the wiring. "Looks good here. Is the monitor plugged in?"

Howell looked behind the monitor. "Shit." He turned it around. All the wires had been yanked from the back. He picked up a phone on the table and put it to his ear. "Dead. Someone didn't want us using this again."

"Doesn't matter," Jen said. "Butler's got the thing bugged. He said they started listening in on our last call with Dr. Cartwright."

"What?" Mark said.

Something bumped into the wall by the door. Zeke jumped up and positioned himself beside the door, drawing his katana. Mark put a finger to his lips and pulled his pistol.

No more bumps on the wall, but stealthy footsteps instead.

Jen moved to the window and peeked through the blinds. Trucks with flashing red and blue lights were parked at the curb. Several shadowy figures ran toward the window. "Cops out here."

Howell reached under the conference table and stood up with a shotgun. He holstered his pistol and jacked a shell into the shotgun's chamber. "We're going to have to fight our way out of here."

"Damn," Jen said. "Got any more shit stashed around here?"

Howell shrugged. "Planted it there before you came in. Just in case."

Zeke looked back at Mark and whispered, "I don't want to kill humans, especially soldiers."

A lump settled in Jen's gut. "I'm with Zeke, but it's either we go all-out, or get captured and let Butler turn us into his undead shock troops. We'll kill a lot more people then."

"He's turning people into zombies?" Howell asked.

Jen nodded. "You know Captain Beal?"

"Beal went missing on patrol." Howell's face hardened. "We kill a few MPs or kill thousands or millions of civilians because we didn't get the information to Dr. Cartwright. It sucks, but I know what I'm going to do."

Mark chewed his lower lip. *This is hitting him where he lives—killing innocents.*

Mark nodded slowly. "So we escape from here. Then what?"

"I've got a blue crew cab truck parked by the chow hall's outside exit. Keys are in it and the tank's full. When we get out of this room, go right and get your asses to the chow hall."

"You leave your keys in your truck?" Zeke asked.

Howell nodded. "By Colonel Butler's order, keys are left in all vehicles on base in case there's an attack and the vehicle is needed."

"Are you coming with us?" Jen asked.

"I've still got a job to do here," Howell said. "I need to relay your information to Dr. Cartwright and keep an eye on Morgan." He licked his lips. "As long as none of these MP's survive, my cover's intact."

"How can you watch Morgan when he's locked up on the fifth floor?" Zeke asked.

Howell shrugged. "He's either there or at his residence across from the base chapel. I bugged it. He hasn't said shit yet, but he'll slip up. It's only a matter of time."

Jen drew her Beretta. "I think we're out of time." A drop of sweat rolled down her cheek. "How do we get this party going?"

Something banged against the door twice. "This is the military police. By order of Colonel Butler, base commander, all civilians are to surrender to us and be placed in protective custody."

Protective, my ass. Jen opened her mouth to tell them so, but Howell shoved his hand over her mouth. "Not the time for a smart-ass comment," he whispered.

Jen nodded and he removed his hand.

"This is Sergeant Howell, Colonel Butler's adjutant. I have the suspects in custody and could use your help in walking them out."

Howell nodded to Mark, who opened the dead bolt and stepped back.

"I've got their weapons secured," Howell said, raising the shotgun to his shoulder. "Request your assistance in moving the prisoners."

Jen knelt behind the conference table, propping her arms on it. She lined up the sights with the door, took a deep breath, then slowly exhaled.

The door burst open.

22

J en fired at the MP in the doorway. He fell to the hallway floor, clamping his hands on his neck, blood spurting between his fingers. Two more MPs rushed through the doorway and Howell's shotgun went off. One of them staggered backward with a shredded chest. The other aimed her pistol at Jen.

Standing behind the door, Zeke stepped out and brought his katana down in an overhead swing, severing the MP's hands. The MP screamed and fell back into the hallway.

Gunfire shattered the window behind Jen. She hit the floor, facing the window. A pistol poked through the blinds, and she fired six rounds in a diagonal pattern. An MP flopped into the room, bringing the blinds down with him. He looked dead, so Jen put a bullet in the back of his head.

Yelling came from the hallway. The first two MPs to be shot had turned. Gunshots went wild, chipping wood from the doorway trim and shattering a ceiling light.

"Now," Jen said. "While they're busy with their friends." She leapt onto the conference room table and jumped off the other side. Streaking out of the room, she went right. A zombie MP had already ripped the throat out of one of his buddies and pressed against the other. The human MP screamed for help. Jen ran past him.

She reached a T intersection in the hall and took a left toward the chow hall. She glanced back just before she went around the corner. Howell was a few feet behind her, and Mark and Zeke had just passed the MPs. The screaming MP had gone silent as his buddy chowed down on his shoulder.

Jen and Howell burst into the chow hall at the same time. Half the tables were occupied, with most of the soldiers on their feet and watching the doorway in alarm. All eyes swiveled to the newcomers. Howell stopped and held out his arm, causing Jen to halt. "What the hell are we waiting for?" she asked.

She turned back to the hallway. *Where the hell are Mark and Zeke?*

A sergeant at a table near the entrance stood. "Sergeant Howell, what's with the shotgun?"

Other soldiers murmured.

Mark rushed into the chow hall, his breathing heavy. "What are you waiting for? Go."

Zeke backed in through the doorway as his katana danced in front of him, keeping a zombie MP back.

Jen yelled, "This way." She took off for the exit, but a stout soldier stepped out in front of her. She aimed at his crotch and fired. The shot missed, but it was enough to make the soldier rethink his strategy as he dived out of the way.

Jen hit the glass doors and pushed them open. Mark and Howell slipped out.

"Where's the truck?" Mark asked.

Howell pointed to the right. "There."

The zombie MPs spilled into the chow hall, with Zeke still battling one of them.

"You two go and get it started," Jen said. "I'll get Zeke."

Jen sprinted for the ninja. "Zeke!"

The zombies had split up and attacked diners. Zeke still sparred with the zombie MP with the shredded chest. The zombie stayed just out of range of the katana, looking for an opening.

Jen aimed at the damned thing's head and pulled the trigger. It dropped to the floor with a hole just behind its temple. Zeke spun around. "That one was mine and Betty's."

She pulled on his arm. "Come on, D'Artagnan. Your carriage awaits."

Soldiers attacked in the dining hall were beginning to turn as Jen and Zeke dashed through the crowd. Jen ran into the back of a zombie. When it lunged at her, its head burst in a spray of blood, brains, and bone. Howell stood at the door, smoke coming from the shotgun's barrel. A zombie soldier charged at him. "Howell," Jen yelled. "Look out."

Howell brought up the shotgun just as the zombie leapt on him, driving him to the floor. He kept its snapping jaws from his face. Jen pulled her axe and swung, cleaving its head just above an ear.

She pushed it to the side and gave Howell a hand up. "I owe you one," he said.

A squad of armed soldiers burst into the chow hall and took down several zombies.

"Get out of here," Howell said.

"Call Cartwright," Jen said. "Tell her Butler plans to attack Washington."

Howell waved her off. "Go."

Jen dashed to the idling truck a few yards outside the door. Zeke held the door open and she dove in. Zeke landed on her a second later. The vehicle took off, the force of it closing the door.

Jen pushed on Zeke. "Want to give me some space?"

Zeke took a seat and helped Jen up.

The truck sped toward the flight line. "Where are we going?" Jen asked.

Mark glanced at her. "Our plane. We're getting the hell out of here."

The sun peeked over the horizon, bathing the base in light and shadows. Mark drove the truck to the flight line and steered it toward the northeast end, where they'd left the plane.

As they got closer, a dozen blue and red flashing lights showed up behind them. "Shit," Mark said. "We've got half the base chasing us."

Jen pointed ahead. "Then there's the other half." Another eight sets of lights approached them from ahead.

"Where the hell do we go?" Mark asked.

"Ram the front gate," Zeke said.

Mark turned the wheel and the truck careened across the runway. "We'll never make it that far."

"What about the opening in the unfinished wall?" Jen said.

"But aren't there fences there to keep zombies out?" Mark asked.

"You got a better idea?"

Sirens blared from behind them. Jen looked back. Two pickup trucks and a Humvee raced after them. The Humvee had a gunner. "They've got a machine gun on that Humvee."

Mark glanced in the mirror. "M-60. It could be a lot worse. Could be a .50 cal."

"Right," Jen said. "So I die from a big bullet up my ass instead of a huge bullet up my ass. Sounds like a deal."

They hit the grass on the other side of the runway and bounced toward the wall opening. The construction crews still had lights on the wall and their equipment in action. Jen checked their pursuers. Not falling back, but not getting closer.

Mark jerked the steering wheel to weave between a front-end loader and a dump truck. He pulled it back to avoid a group of workers, then straightened it out. "They won't shoot with all these construction workers around."

He pointed through the windshield. "Look at the fence. See the opening for the first fence on the far left? We go in there, hang a right, and the second fence's opening is about seventy-five percent of the way across. It's like a maze."

"I'll trust you," Jen said. "But I say we just ram through it."

The truck rattled over the uneven ground. "Here we go." Mark hit the brakes and slowed to a crawl, then made a hard right turn. The engine roared as he accelerated, then slowed and made a left before speeding up again.

The M60 on the Humvee opened up.

"Hold on," Mark said. "One more to go."

Bullets sang as they passed over the truck. Mark slammed on the brakes for the last opening and took the turn, ripping the passenger's side-view mirror off on the gate. The back window shattered and he floored the accelerator, breaking out into clear, flat land.

Jen and Zeke bumped fists. "We made it," Zeke said.

"Don't celebrate yet," Jen said. "We escaped Butler only to end up in a zombie war zone."

23

The truck bounced over the uneven ground. Mark could barely keep the wheel straight. He steered for a road several yards away, where the truck jumped the curb and the ride smoothed out. "Damn," Jen said. "My ass is going to hurt for the next week."

Mark steered around an abandoned vehicle. "So what the hell did you find out? What's Butler up to that's so dangerous?"

"I'm not sure you'll believe me."

Zeke settled back into the seat. "I'd believe you if you told me Butler was going to raise Godzilla from the sea."

Snickering, Jen said, "Thanks. But it's not that far off."

Zeke straightened.

"Just tell us," Mark said. "After all we've been through and the crazy shit we've seen, I'm not sure more crazy shit wouldn't make sense."

"Morgan has been experimenting on zombies." Jen cleared her throat. "Butler wants to build himself an undead army that he commands to march on Washington, D.C., and take over the government."

Mark raised an eyebrow. "Based on the way you've acted since you found that out, I'm guessing you think that's possible."

"I saw it with my own eyes. They tapped our last conversation with Cartwright and heard our observations about the leaders. The plan is to control the leaders, which allows them to control the drones."

Zeke sat up. "I saw a movie like that. They put collars on them and made them do stuff."

"They have a helmet," Jen said. "It's like a bike helmet. They put it on the leader and they hit a remote control button that hurts the zombie. I've never seen one cringe before."

"A zombie in pain?" Mark asked. "How?"

"Morgan said the helmet emits localized EMP waves or something like that," Jen said. "But the bottom line is he can get the leader to do what he wants, and he says the leader can control ten thousand drones."

Mark whistled. "We need to find a way to call Cartwright."

Jen frowned. A dozen zombies stumbled around at the intersection ahead. Beyond it lay a subdivision. "We're the only ones who can prevent Butler's plans. It'll be too late for anyone else to act."

Mark swerved around two zombies. Another ran at the truck and bounced off the bumper. "I still think we should try to get word to Cartwright."

"Why not do both?" Zeke said. "Contact her, then go kick Butler's ass. I'm up for that."

"What do you say?" Mark asked.

Jen shrugged. "OK. We try one place to see if we can call out. But it's got to be somewhere we can hide for now.

Tonight, we go after Butler, no matter if we've contacted Cartwright or not."

"OK," Mark said. "We want to find a place that's likely to have a generator and some other form of communication, like a radio."

Zeke held up a walkie-talkie. "Here's a radio."

"Need a stronger one than that to reach Atlanta," Jen said.

They'd arrived at Route 902, and Mark stopped at the intersection. "Which direction?"

A sign ahead told them to go left for Spokane and right for Medical Lake. Mark jabbed a finger at the sign. "There's a good place. A hospital. Bet we find a generator and radio there."

Jen squinted. A smaller sign below the other one said Eastern Hospital and had an arrow that pointed right. "Good idea. A hospital should be defensible and have some food."

Mark turned onto Route 902 and followed the signs. As they passed Lefevre Street, Jen pointed past him. "Look."

A thousand or more zombies milled around in front of a school two blocks down. A sign for the high school stood on the corner. "I've had enough of high schools," Jen said.

Mark laughed. "That was pretty intense."

"What?" Zeke asked.

"In Anchorage," Jen said. "When you were babysitting Trip and his gang. We had to lose a mega horde by driving through a high school."

"Damn," Zeke said. "I missed some fun stuff."

They came to the intersection of North Howard Street. A sign for Eastern Hospital pointed them to the left. Mark followed the road down to a lake.

Jen pointed across the lake. "I'll bet that's the hospital."

A long multistoried brown building, partially hidden by trees, stood atop a small hill.

Mark rubbed the stubble on his chin. "Looks a bit institutional. Even for a hospital."

He turned onto the road and followed it around the lake and up a gradual slope through the trees. It led to a series of buildings, the largest being the brown one they'd spotted across the lake. "Eastern State Hospital" was engraved over the main doorway. Most of the buildings were brick, and it looked like one of those places you'd see the ghost chaser shows on TV investigate.

Zeke smiled. "Pretty creepy place."

"I don't think this is your typical hospital." Mark pointed to a fenced-in area. "That looks like some kind of recreation area."

"Are they trying to keep people out, or in?" Jen asked.

Mark pulled into a parking lot. "If nothing else, it's huge and Butler would have a hard time finding us here."

He parked between a green-and-tan jeep and a shiny black minivan. "No zombies so far."

He turned off the truck and hopped out. "But there's a lot of room inside that building to hold them. Don't get complacent."

Jen climbed out of the truck and checked her weapons' loads. She switched out magazines on her pistol and shoved it back in the holster.

"Can I get some help?" Zeke pulled two stuffed backpacks from the back seat.

"What are those?" Jen asked.

Zeke plopped them down on the asphalt. "Goodie bags. This is where I got the radio. They've got extra ammo and food and shit." He jerked a thumb to the canopy on the back of the truck. "I looked back there and found a few more."

Mark unzipped one and rifled through the contents. "Nice. We'll have to thank Howell for this."

"We should move with the bare essentials for now," Jen said. "We can lock the truck and this stuff'll be here when we want it."

Zeke and Mark tossed the packs back in and locked the doors. Jen crossed to the nearest building entrance, two tall doors in an imposing entryway. She waited for Mark and Zeke to catch up, then pressed the old-style thumb latch and pulled the door open.

Light spilled into the entry way, across a dirty tile floor. A flight of stairs with an old-fashioned scrolled railing led to a landing and another flight of steps. The hallway extended into the gloom on either side.

A counter that reminded Jen of a hotel reception desk in old Westerns stood off to the side. Jen ducked behind it, shining her light on the paperwork sitting on a shelf. She picked some up. One was a doctor's note on a patient. Next to diagnosis, it said Paranoid Schizophrenia.

Jen straightened and laid the papers on the counter. "I know why this place looks so creepy and unhospital-like."

Zeke slid his katana from the sheath strapped to his back and faced the darkness of the corridor on their left.

"You see something?" Mark asked.

"Not sure," Zeke said. "Maybe."

Jen cleared her throat and Mark turned toward her. "This is a mental hospital," she said.

Zeke put a hand up. "Listen."

Jen strained to hear anything from the hallways. The stairs. She shook her head. "Don't hear anything in here."

Zeke raced to the door. "Not in here. Out there."

Jen and Mark joined him at the door. The unmistakable *thup thup* of helicopter rotors came closer. Jen pulled the door closed, plunging the lobby into darkness. Each of them turned on a flashlight.

"Think they're looking for us?" she asked.

Mark grunted. "I never heard of them coming this way before. Always to Spokane. And since we escaped heading south, I think it's a good bet they aren't just sightseeing."

The muffled sound of the rotors got louder. *Are they going to land here?*

Jen cracked the door open. The helicopter hovered above a small building a couple hundred yards away. "Why would they think we're here? Are they checking out the whole town?"

The helicopter rose and flew over them toward the lake and the town. Jen opened both doors and set the doorstop. "At least this will give us a little light in here. Let's check this place out. Medical or mental hospital, they could both have a generator and maybe a radio."

She pulled out her axe. "I'll take lead."

"I've got rear." Zeke took a couple of practice swings with his katana.

Jen led them to the right, the lights from her beam and Mark's tracing across the walls and floor. The first door on their right stood open. Standing back from it, she shined her beam inside. Desks, chairs, and computers. Nothing looked disturbed.

Moving on, they cleared all the first floor rooms on that side of the building, ending up in a small break room with soda and snack machines. Jen plopped down on a chair. "It'd take us a couple of days to clear this whole damn building. We don't have that kind of time."

Mark bit his lip. "Agreed. Although I don't like it, we'll have to take more of a risk."

He shined his light on the snack machine. "Potato chips.

I could use a few of those." He swung the beam to the soda machine. "And a cola. Even warm, it'd hit the spot."

Zeke pointed to a high energy drink. "I down those things like water when I'm in an all-nighter RPG binge with my friends."

"RPG?" Mark said. "Is that like your FPS?"

Jen groaned. "Let's get back to business. There's no power, so the machines won't work."

"I'm sure your axe could shatter the glass," Mark said. "Then we can take what we want."

"Are you nuts? That racket would bring every zombie hiding in this wing."

Mark smiled. "Exactly. Flush them out at one time. Like you said, we don't have time to go door to door."

Why didn't I think of that?

"Stand back." Jen stood in front of the snack machine and cocked the axe back. *One, two, three.* She swung the blade, shattering the glass into big chunks that fell away. She repeated her actions on the soda machine.

Mark ran to the doorway and cocked his head. "We've got company. And a lot of it."

Mark eased the door closed and Jen pushed the fallen soda machine toward it. Zeke and Mark helped and they had it blocking the door in seconds.

Jen found a corner table and laid her weapons out on it. The footsteps seemed like they were everywhere—in the hall, the floor above, and on the other side of the walls behind her. It was like the building was infested with big-ass mice.

Zeke and Mark joined her in the corner. Mark knelt and had his rife to his shoulder. Zeke took a defensive stance and had his katana ready to taste zombie blood.

The stampede continued and gave no signs of stopping. Jen's watch told her it'd been ten minutes. *Are they just running around in circles out there?*

One of them ran into the door every minute or so. It would rattle and Jen would aim at it, but no effort was made to breach the room. The zombies had no idea they were there.

Thirty minutes passed, and Zeke and Mark sat down,

deciding the risk of attack was low. Even at rest, though, they kept their weapons close and were ready to jump into action.

Jen leaned against the wall, the vibrations helping her keep track of the zombies' tempo. It seemed to her it had slowed a bit.

She stood, and Mark and Zeke looked at her, Mark with his trademark one eyebrow raised, and Zeke with his smirk and curious eyes.

Jen crept to the window and peeked through the blinds. A number of the zombies had made it outside, where some continued to run as if they chased something, and others had slowed and wandered.

She went back to the table. "It's slowing," she whispered. "It reminds me of when you disturb a wasp's nest. They'll go batshit for a while, then calm down."

She leaned against the wall. The vibrations had died to where she could make out individual footsteps. She closed her eyes and concentrated. *Another one dropped out. And another.*

Five minutes later, one set of footsteps was all that remained.

"It's pretty much done," she whispered.

Mark kept his voice low. "That's all well and good, but how many are just standing around in the hallway, ready to sound the alarm?"

Zeke stood. "With no window on the door, there's only one way to tell."

Jen snuck to the window and scanned the road and parking lot. *Damn.* "All the ones that were out here a while ago are gone."

Mark joined her. "If your analogy of the wasp's nest is

right, then they're all back in here." He sighed. "This building won't work. Too many."

Jen raised the blinds and pointed across the road to a smaller one-story building. "How about that?"

"Easier to clear and control," Mark said.

Zeke opened the window and hopped onto the grass beneath it. He crouched, his hand on the katana's handle, and scanned the area. "All clear."

Jen crawled through the window and walked with him to the smaller building's door. A plaque next to it read "Auxiliary Supply."

She turned the knob and pulled the door open, rearing the axe over her shoulder.

Mark rushed in and shined his flashlight beam to the left, while Zeke pointed his to the right.

Boxes and office furniture lined the walls. "Guess this is their equivalent to a junk drawer," Jen said. She walked past Zeke and pointed her beam at a closed wooden door painted institutional green.

"Might as well start here." She turned the knob and cracked the door open, shining the light through the slit opening.

"More damn furniture." The beam caught a desk with a cushy faux leather chair behind it. Nothing moved, so she pushed the door wider and played the beam over the room. A couple of desks, computers, and phones gathered dust, while stacks of paper flowed from inboxes and a sorry-looking coffee maker sat on a counter next to a sink. "That's got to be one of the dreariest things I've ever seen," Jen said.

Zeke pushed past her. "I swore I'd never have a nine-to-five desk job. Now you know why."

Mark sat in the plushy chair, leaned back, and rested his feet on the desk. "I don't know. Doesn't feel too bad to me."

Jen and Zeke laughed. *Nice to see Mark let his hair down for once.*

A bump came from the far wall. All the light beams shined on it. Nothing but a short bookcase.

The bump sounded again. "Guess we have a wasp's nest here, too," Mark said.

"Can't be as many," Zeke said. "This place wouldn't hold them."

Jen had her ear pressed to the wall. "More than one. They're in the next room."

She crept into the hallway and to the next door down. The damn things bumped against the door, rattling it in its frame.

Mark appeared next to her. "If we're quiet, they shouldn't get too stirred up."

Jen studied the furniture crowding the hallway. "I've got a better idea. Help me out."

She grabbed a chair and placed it next to another just outside the door where the zombies stumbled around. "Keep the path wide at this end, then make it more narrow further down the corridor."

Mark placed a desk next to the chair. He smiled. "Brilliant."

Zeke pitched in, and soon Jen stood back and studied their work. The piles of furniture against the wall were stacked five feet high and created a funnel with the wide end next to the door and the narrow end twenty feet down the hall. "I think we're ready," Jen said.

She pulled her axe from her belt and approached the door. She nodded at Zeke and Mark at the other end of the funnel. "Get ready. I'll be running my ass off."

Mark stood on one side of the hallway with his mace and Zeke took the other, his katana at the ready. Jen grasped the doorknob. Something bumped it and she pulled the door open.

A zombie in a lab coat with a tie glared at her, his yellow eyes piercing. She caught a glance of multiple pairs of yellow eyes in the darkness of the room before she sprinted down the hall.

The lab coat zombie dashed after her. He nearly grabbed the back of her shirt just as she reached Zeke and Mark. "Duck," Mark yelled.

Jen dove for the floor behind Mark, who swung his mace upward and connected with the zombie's jaw, shattering it. It stumbled, giving Zeke enough time to cleanly behead it.

The undead poured out of the room and raced for the humans, but jammed up at the funnel's end. With only room for one at a time, they couldn't overwhelm their prey.

Jen, Mark, and Zeke got into a rhythm. Jen would crack a skull open with her axe, then drag it forward as Mark caved in another's head. As it fell, Zeke stepped in and separated the next zombie from its head. When the last one stumbled forward, Zeke raised his katana. "Me and Betty have this one." He waited until the zombie was within range and sliced, but only got the blade halfway through its neck. It stumbled back, its head tilted to the side.

Zeke raised his sword and paused. "What the hell?"

The blade had snapped in half. "Betty!"

The zombie lunged for him, and Mark pulled him back. "Keep your head in the game."

Jen planted her blade in the zombie's scalp and it dropped to the floor with a thud. "Damn, Zeke. You've got to pay attention."

"Looked like about fifty of them," Mark said.

Zeke picked up the broken-off blade and held it and the

katana up. "I knew it wouldn't last." He looked at Jen. "It wasn't a real katana, you know."

No shit. Jen put her hand up. "Listen."

Mark tilted his head, then smiled. "Nothing."

"Let's check this place out." Jen stepped over a body and strode down the hall.

Twenty minutes later they had cleared the building, finding only one more zombie, a janitor stuck in his closet.

"I think the break room's a good place to set up," Mark said. "Two doors, easily defensible, plus it has water and food."

Jen nodded. "We should get those backpacks in here and plan our next move."

"You get those," Mark said. "I'm going to check all the phones."

Ten minutes later Mark lumbered into the break room. "Any luck?" Zeke asked.

Mark collapsed in a chair. "No, I checked every damn phone." He looked at a wall phone situated next to a silent refrigerator. "Except that one."

Jen picked it up and shook her head. "Sorry."

Zeke pushed past her and grabbed the refrigerator handle. "Wonder what's in here?"

Jen put a hand across his chest. "Don't you dare. Whatever's in there is guaranteed to knock us over with its stench."

Mark dumped one of the backpacks onto a table. He picked up two walkie-talkies. "Jen, Zeke."

They walked over and he tossed one to each of them. "Why do we need these?" Zeke asked. "I thought we were going to stick together."

Mark emptied the other backpack and fished another radio out of the pile. "You never know if we'll get separated." He turned his radio on and adjusted the channel until voices came from the speaker. "Besides, we can listen in on Butler."

"Hotel One to Command One. No sign of targets in sector twelve."

Butler's voice came over the airwaves, the noise of a helicopter's interior in the background. "Roger, Hotel One. Proceed to sector twenty-one."

"Roger."

"Command One to all units. This mission will continue until the targets are located and neutralized. If this has not been done by nightfall, we'll pick right back up in the morning."

A series of "Rogers" followed.

"Hotel Four to Command One. Request permission to deviate and recon for Zulus in the west."

"Negative, Hotel Four. You have your orders."

Zeke found a bag of chips in the cupboard, tore it open, and stuffed a few in his mouth.

Mark turned off the radio. "Butler's taking a risk not sending out his recon. If a huge horde from Seattle or Portland heads this way, he may not have much warning."

"Wish I had a map with the sectors identified," Jen said. "Then I'd know where his men were." She kicked the wall. "But it wouldn't matter. How can we lure him in without his entire army coming along?"

"Mmff-crir." Bits of potato chips fell out of Zeke's mouth.

"Wait," Jen said. "I think the great Oracle is about to grace us with his wisdom."

Zeke swallowed, making exaggerated expressions. "I said, you just need to have something he wants and doesn't want to lose."

"What the hell would that be?" Mark asked. "He wants us, but he'd be just as happy if we killed ourselves."

Jen snapped her fingers. "You're a genius, Zeke. I know exactly what he'd want."

"I know I'm going to regret asking this," Mark said, "but what would that be?"

"Dr. Morgan. We're going to kidnap him tonight."

25

Clouds slid in front of the quarter moon as Jen parked the black minivan between the last two houses at the end of the road.

"This is the dumbest idea I've ever heard," Mark said. "Break into the base we just escaped from."

"That's why it's perfect," Jen said. "Who would expect someone to be dumb enough to try it?"

Zeke slid the side door open and jumped out. "I love using my ninja skills. This'll be a blast."

Mark sighed and opened his door. "If they make me a zombie, I'm going to eat your face off."

"Deal," Jen said.

Zeke was harder to spot in the shadows than normal. In addition to his black ninja costume, Mark had applied some camo face paint around Zeke's eyes that he'd found in one of the packs.

Jen raised a pair of binoculars and scanned the wall. Two guards stood on the other side of the fence. Lights on the outside of the wall lit up the area twenty yards out from the fence.

She handed the binoculars to Mark. "Just as I'd hoped." She pointed to the gap. "Look there."

Mark adjusted the focus, then gave a low whistle. "Butler's pulled all the combat engineers from finishing the wall. Bet he's got them out looking for us, too. But only two guards? What if a horde attacks?"

"Who knows what that crazy ass is thinking?" Jen said. "Maybe they're just there to raise the alarm. The fence could hold back a decent horde long enough for reinforcements." Jen stretched her arms and shook them out. "Either way, if we make a straight line to it from here, there's a narrow dark strip where we can get almost all the way to the wall."

"And if we're caught out there in the open," Mark said, "we're screwed."

Jen pulled the rifle off her shoulder. "Let's go. In and out."

"What if he's not at his quarters?" Mark asked. "What if he's in Area 51?"

Jen shrugged. "Then we think up a plan B." She crouched and crept onto the field, the dead grass crunching under her feet. Mark caught up with her and she glanced back to find Zeke, but he'd disappeared. *Freaking ninja.*

Halfway across the field, Mark's arm shot out across her chest. "Get down," he whispered.

Jen dropped prone on the ground and had her rifle to her shoulder. She scanned the field in front of her through the rifle's iron sights, but nothing moved.

"Why are we lying here?" she whispered.

"Listen," Mark said. "Ahead and to the right."

Irregular footsteps crunching the grass came from that direction, and they headed their way. *Zombie.*

She pulled her axe from her belt. "You got your mace?"

"Yup," Mark whispered. "You ready to go?"

"Always."

"On three," Mark said. "One, two, three."

Jen hopped to her feet and dashed into the shadows, staying low. If she ran into the zombie in the dark, it would be harder for it to bite her if it had to bend over to do it.

A *thud* and an *oof* that reminded Jen of a football player making a tackle came from her right.

"Go high," Mark said.

A solid shadow stood in front of her. Jen wound her arm back and rushed it, swinging toward the top of the shadow as she passed.

The axe bit into bone. After all the zombies she'd sent to hell, she could tell what she hit just by the feel of it.

The zombie fell, taking her axe with it.

"Mark," she said. "Where are you?"

His voice came from beside her. "I ran into the damn thing. Thanks for taking it out."

"No problem." She felt around on the ground until she found the zombie. She held her breath and fumbled for the axe handle, then yanked it out.

Jen rose away from the dead creature and started breathing again. "Hope there aren't any more."

She peered toward the wall opening. The two guards walked their post, making no indication they'd heard the scuffle. "Where the hell is Zeke?" she asked.

Mark cleared his throat. "Hard to see shit out here. Better stay close."

"Those guards are easy to see," Jen said. Something moved in the shadows a few yards from the guard shack. *What the hell?*

The guards huddled and one lit a match, pressing it to the end of a cigarette in the other guard's mouth. A shadow broke away from the gloom just outside the light's reach and crept to the edge of the fence. The guards took no notice as one of them laughed while the other talked.

Jen squinted. *Is that...?* "Zeke?"

Mark groaned. "What the hell is he doing?"

Jen jogged toward the gap, well out of the light's range. Ninja or no, Zeke was pushing it.

Zeke picked something up from the ground and climbed halfway up the fence. Only several yards away, the guards were so involved in conversation, neither had noticed the ninja.

When Zeke reached the top of the fence, he tossed an object toward the other end of the fence. The laughter stopped and both guards raised their weapons, pointing them into the gloom and away from Zeke.

Jen slowed, and Mark caught up to her. "We're getting too close to the light," she said.

Zeke jumped from the top of the fence and landed like a cat. The soldiers still had their backs to him. One of them said something to the other, who shook his head.

Zeke removed the scabbard from his back as he approached the guards like a leopard ready to leap on its prey.

"Come on. Come on," Mark said.

One of the guards turned halfway toward Zeke.

Shit. They see him and he'll be gunned down in the open. Jen lit out toward the light.

Mark let out a soft "What the hell?"

Jen yelled, "Hey, Asshole. I'm over here."

Awash in the bright lights, she shielded her eyes with her hand.

"Stop," one of the guards yelled. "Hands up."

Jen slowed, but kept walking. *Got to give Zeke time.*

A distinct *click click* of chambers being loaded made her heart skip a beat.

"One more step and we shoot."

26

J en threw her hands in the air and froze in place, her breath coming in shallow gasps.

"Come forward slowly," a soldier said.

Jen took a step, paused, then took another. She squinted. Best as she could see, the guards' attention was fully on her. *Good.*

Ten yards away, a shadow raced toward the soldiers. One of them glanced over his shoulder and yelled. Zeke had the katana's handle in both hands and swung it, scabbard and all, slamming it into the first guard's temple. He collapsed. As the other soldier swung his gun around, Zeke slid in low, taking the guard out at his knees. The soldier fell, losing his grip on the rifle, and it clattered to the ground. Zeke swept it up and pounded the fallen guard in the forehead with the butt.

Jen broke into a run, and Mark raced past her seconds later. Zeke opened a gate in the fence and stood there as calm as could be, waiting for the others to catch up.

Mark grabbed Zeke as he passed through the gate and dragged him into the shadows.

Jen closed the gate behind her and joined them. "What the hell was that?"

"Mark said we shouldn't kill any of the soldiers if we don't have to, right? But we had to get in here, didn't we? I just took care of it."

"Dammit, Zeke," Mark said. "You can't—"

"Wait," Jen said. "Why be surprised? This is who Zeke is, and he did get us in without having to seriously hurt anyone."

Mark grunted. "Still, we need to work as a team."

"Zeke," Jen said, "promise us you won't pull this bullshit again."

Zeke sighed. "OK."

"Good enough," Jen said. "We don't have time to sit here and talk about it. Let's go around the flight line."

"I'm lead." Mark hustled off.

Zeke tapped her on the shoulder. "I've got it back here."

Catching up with Mark, Jen stayed a few feet behind him. Zeke didn't make a sound, and she had to glance back every couple of minutes to make sure he was still there.

The flight line had minimal lights, which made it easy to skirt around without being seen.

Mark stopped on the side of a dark maintenance hangar. "Should we get transportation now?" He pointed at a Humvee parked across the access road.

"Perfect." Jen climbed into the driver's side. "And thanks to Butler, the keys are in it." Mark and Zeke hopped in. Jen started the engine and put the truck in gear, pulling out. "Anyone know where the chapel is?"

"Take your second left," Zeke said.

Mark glanced at him. "How do you know where it is?"

"I've gone out every night and scouted the whole base."

Mark looked at Jen and raised an eyebrow. *Zeke never fails to surprise.*

Jen made the turn. "Go two more blocks and take a right," Zeke said. "Morgan's place will be two blocks past that on the left."

The truck turned onto a street with single-family houses. All were dark, except one up on the left. A single guard stood watch out front. "Were there any guards before?" Jen asked.

"Just the one up front," Zeke answered. "We should come in from the rear, though, in case security's been increased."

As they passed the front of the house, the guard raised a hand. Jen did the same. She drove a few more blocks then turned off the road and approached the house from the rear, turning the truck around before stopping. "Just in case we need to get out of here quick."

They gathered in the shadows of a tall hedge. "Zeke should go first," Mark said. "Just scouting. Then report back."

Zeke gave them a thumbs-up, then padded off. He disappeared like a ghost between two trees.

Jen pulled her pistol. "Hope I don't have to use this."

"If you do, it means all hell's broken loose."

Minutes passed and all Jen heard were crickets chirping and her own shallow breathing.

A shadow detached from a fence and crept their way. Jen raised the pistol. *Probably Zeke, but just in case...*

The shadow disappeared ten yards out. Mark cleared his throat. "Zeke," he said. "Answer now, or I'll shoot."

"It's me." Zeke's voice came from beside Jen and she jumped back, nearly tripping. "Holy shit, you scared the piss out of me."

"Sorry."

"What's the scoop?" Mark asked.

"Only the one guard," Zeke said. "House is completely dark inside, but the bathroom window on the first floor is unlocked. Doesn't move real smooth, but I can get it all the way up without making noise."

Damn. He's handy to have around.

"First thing is to take out the guard," Mark said. "Then we go inside."

"I've got a plan," Jen said.

Ten minutes later, Jen pulled the Humvee to a stop in front of the house. She rolled down the window and the guard walked over.

"Kinda cold out here," Jen said. "I'm heading in for some coffee. Can I bring you a cup?"

Still a few yards away, the guard smiled. "Thanks. I appreciate..." He squinted at her and drew his pistol. "Why are you wearing camo paint?"

A beefy arm wrapped around the guard's neck, causing him to drop the gun. Mark kept the pressure on until the guard stopped struggling. He dragged the unconscious soldier into the bushes. Jen looked around. "Where's Zeke?" she whispered.

"Right here." Zeke stood in the open doorway. "Let's go," he whispered. "Morgan's asleep. Guy snores like a freight train."

Jen and Mark followed him inside and down a hallway. Snorting sounds came from behind the last door. *Zeke wasn't kidding.*

Mark eased the door open and crept to the side of the bed. Zeke joined him. Mark nodded at Jen and she flipped the light switch.

Morgan cried out. Blinking from the sudden light, Jen pointed her gun in his general direction. "I'd just as soon kill you right here, so if you do anything other than what you're told, you die. And the bullet won't go in your head, so you could be one of Butler's puppets."

"I'll do what you want," Morgan said in a shaky voice.

Jen's eyes adjusted to the light. Morgan had curled up at the head of the bed. Mark grabbed his arm and yanked him to his feet. "Get dressed."

Morgan looked at Jen.

"Oh, for shit's sake." Jen backed into the hallway and closed the door, then snuck to the living room and peered out the front window.

An MP truck approached and slowed down. The passenger shined a flashlight beam on the truck they'd left out front, then at the house. Jen ducked just in time. She looked back out and the truck took off, turning a block down the road. Steady red brake lights reflected off a house window. *They're not leaving.*

Jen ran to the room and flung the door open. "We've got an MP patrol outside and I'll bet they've called for backup."

27

Mark pushed Morgan's face into the bed and pulled his arms behind him. Morgan cried out, "Don't break my arms."

Zeke held up a pair of zip tie handcuffs. "Found these in the truck."

Mark put them on Morgan and pulled him to his feet. "Come on."

Jen led them to the front window. Red and blue lights flashed down the street. MPs, their guns drawn, took cover a block over. "We've got a bunch of MPs on the right." She looked down the other end of the street. No movement. "But the left looks clear."

Zeke opened the door and Mark walked out, pushing Morgan in front of him. He held his pistol to the doctor's head.

An MP shouted, "Drop your weapons."

"You're going to let us leave," Mark yelled. "Or Morgan's dead."

Jen and Zeke stayed behind Mark as they moved toward the truck.

"I repeat. Drop your weapons or we'll open fire."

The lights of two more MP trucks turned a corner in the distance. "Shit," Mark said. "New plan."

"What new plan?" Jen asked.

"You take Morgan in the truck. Zeke and I will cover you and keep these guys busy."

"Bullshit," Jen said.

"I don't want to die," Morgan moaned.

"Mark's right," Zeke said. "It's the only way. We'll distract them so you can get Morgan somewhere secure, then we'll meet up with you later."

This whole thing's going to shit. "Where?"

"That first building downtown they left us on," Mark said. "Now take Morgan. No time for chitchat."

Jen grasped Morgan's upper arm and pulled him toward the truck.

"This is your last warning," the MP yelled. "Drop your weapons and release Dr. Morgan."

Mark and Zeke ran back to the house, firing several shots toward the MPs. Jen yanked Morgan to the truck and flung the back door open. "Move it, asshole." She shoved him onto the seat and slammed the door.

Bullets pinged off the back of the Humvee as Jen jumped into the driver's seat. A voice called out. "Do not fire on the vehicle. Dr. Morgan is in it."

The front window of the house was already gone. Zeke and Mark fired steadily from the shadows.

Jen started the engine and peeled out. She glanced back at the house. *You assholes better escape or I'll kick your butts.*

She took the next turn hard and heard a thump in the back. "Ow," Morgan said.

Straightening the truck, she floored it, blowing through

stop signs and heading for the flight line. Flashing lights pulled out several blocks back.

"Better hold on, Morgan. It's gonna get rocky."

"I'm still on the floor. Let me get up."

They flew across the flight line, bouncing and shuddering on the uneven ground on the other side. Morgan screamed as he was thrown around in the back. Jen grinned. "Ooo. I bet that's gonna bruise."

The gap fence was lit up like a theater stage, and several soldiers milled around. They looked up as the Humvee zoomed down the slope toward the fence. Jen honked the horn and kept the pedal to the floor. "Hang on, Morgan. We've got a Humvee this time and we're going through that freaking fence."

The soldiers scattered, one diving out of the Humvee's way at the last second. The vehicle hit the fence and the chain link tore right off the posts. The Humvee slowed as it went through the second fence and damn near didn't make it through the third.

Jen goosed the accelerator, turned off her lights, and drove into the darkness. Her pursuers stopped at the ruined fence.

A few minutes later, she turned onto South Graham Road, speeding for the 902 into Spokane. She slammed her fist on the dash.

No way they didn't get caught. And a damn good chance they were shot.

She took the on ramp to the 902. When she checked her rearview mirror, Morgan's face filled it. He had a good bruise on his forehead and his glasses were missing. "What do you think of me so far?" Jen asked. He remained tight-lipped.

She sped up, dodging abandoned vehicles and the occasional zombie. Glancing out the windows and in the rearview mirror every couple of minutes, she strained to hear the sound of approaching rotors. But none came.

Reaching Highway 90, she slowed as the obstacles increased. The sky had gone into a deep blue pre-dawn. *Got to find a place to hole up.*

When they reached the Route 2 interchange, the road cleared. It looked as if someone had gone through with plows and pushed everything to the side.

Morgan leaned back in the seat. "You know the colonel will move heaven and earth to free me."

Jen took the exit to South Division Street and turned north. "I'm counting on it."

Small groups of zombies wandered about. All drones. *All they need is one leader to pick up the thousands wandering the city.*

Morgan straightened in the seat and peered out the window. His voice trembled. "Do you know how many zombies are out here? You can turn a corner and be surrounded by ten thousand."

Jen chuckled. "Wouldn't that be karma if they chewed on the asshole experimenting on them."

"We can't keep driving around the city like this," Morgan said. "We'll draw the wrong kind of attention."

Jen stopped the Humvee. "Shush."

"Don't shush me."

Jen drew her Beretta and pointed it at Morgan's face. "Then shut the fuck up instead."

Morgan went silent. Jen turned off the engine and opened her window. Loose garbage and leaves skittered down the street in the wind. But another sound rose above it. Still in the distance, it grew louder.

Helicopter.

28

J en started the engine and threw it into gear. She knew where she wanted to hide out, and it wasn't far. They zoomed down South Division Street, barely missing an overturned van and plowing over a zombie dog that rushed in front of them. At Second Avenue, Jen took a sharp left and turned off her lights.

She pulled up in front of a long tall building off South Madison Street, turned off the Humvee, and hopped out with her axe in hand. The helicopter was so loud, she expected to see it hovering over her.

Opening the back door, she grabbed Morgan by the upper arm and yanked him out of the vehicle. "Stay right here. I'm your only protection."

Leaning into the front seat, Jen picked up the M4 Zeke had left and threw it over her shoulder.

"You can't do this to me," Morgan said. "I was just following orders."

Jen guided him through a set of glass doors and pulled him toward the stairs. "I suggest you shut the hell up unless you want to attract some of your friendly neighborhood drones."

Morgan's lips tightened.

They stopped on the third floor landing. Had she heard something? Jen pressed an ear against the door. Shambling footsteps. A few, just a few. She put a finger to her lips and jerked her thumb at the door. Morgan nodded. He understood.

Keeping hold of his upper arm, she guided him up the next few flights to the top floor, where a sign welcomed them to the top-rated insurance company in the state. Jen dragged him into an office and sat him behind a desk. "You can cool your heels here while I check things out."

"You can't leave me tied up and alone," Morgan whined. "What if a zombie comes by while you're gone?"

Jen stepped into the hallway. "If you're quiet, they won't know you're here." She closed the door. *Dumbass.*

Methodically working her way from office to office, it took her twenty minutes to clear the floor. She had half a mind to jerk the office door open and see if Morgan would shit his pants, but decided against it. *Don't want to be stuck up here with that and no ventilation.*

She pulled the desk out of the office and shoved it against the door to the stairway. *Won't stop a horde, but it'll keep anything from sneaking up on me.*

Morgan glared at her as she plopped down on a chair next to him. "Butler's going to tear your friends apart if you don't let me go."

Jen's gut ached. *I got them into it and I'll get them back.*

Feeling anything but happy, she nonetheless smiled at Morgan. "As long as I have you, he won't do shit." She pulled the radio off her belt and switched it on.

Nothing came across. She changed the channel. Still nothing. "What channels do they use?"

Morgan slumped back in his seat and shrugged. "How the hell do I know? I need something and I pick up the phone."

Jen scoffed. *Asshole's as useful as a solar-powered flashlight.*

She continued changing the channel. A voice came from the radio on the third try. "Echo Twenty-three to base. Entering Medical Lake."

Keying the mic, she said, "This is a message for Command One. Command One, do you read?"

Silence, then, "Base to unidentified personnel. This is a military-restricted channel. Identify yourself."

"I want to talk to Command One."

"Negative. Identify yourself. You are in violation of emergency martial law orders and will be held accountable."

Jen stood. "Look, asswipe. Butler's already trying to kill me, so I'm not particularly worried about some regulations. I suggest you get that excuse of a colonel on here because I have something he wants."

Weaker voices came across, patrols communicating directly with each other. Then a burst of static. "Base to unidentified personnel. Switch to channel thirty-two."

"Ten-four, good buddy. Keep them smokies off your tail."

Jen moved the dial to the new channel and listened. Nothing but light static. A clear channel? *Doesn't want any of his men hearing this.*

She keyed the mic. "I'm here."

"Seems you and I have a problem." Butler's voice seemed strained, even over the airwaves.

"Yup. How about we make a trade? Give me my folks back and you get Doctor Frankenstein here."

Morgan scowled at her. She kept the mic keyed and kicked him in the shin.

"Ow. Bitch. Get me out of here, Butler."

Jen brought the mic to her lips. "Your guy's still up and kicking. How about I talk to mine?"

"Jen."

"Mark? You and Zeke OK?"

"Yeah. Listen, don't trust—"

"Mark? Can you hear me? Mark?"

Butler's voice came on. She could hear the sneer in it. "Your friends are fine. Where do we make the exchange?"

Morgan gave Jen a puzzled look as she strode from the room and down the hall.

"Where do we make the exchange?" Butler repeated.

Jen peered out a window at the end of the hall. "Remember the hotel roof you dropped us off at?"

"Yes."

The hotel's roof was visible. *Just a block away.* "Bring Mark and Zeke, and you'll get Morgan."

"When?"

"How long will it take you to get here?"

Butler paused.

"An hour."

Shouldn't take more than twenty minutes for him to get here. Son of a bitch is up to something. "Agreed."

The channel went silent. Jen turned the radio off and clipped it back to her belt.

She'd set it up so Butler would land on the hotel and she could see if he was alone, then have him fly over to the building she was in.

Morgan looked up when she entered the office. "So?"

Jen shrugged. "Your boss said he'll be here in an hour. I've got plans to throw him off his game."

Morgan laughed. "You think you're going to outthink a soldier? Little girl, he's already ten moves ahead of you."

Jen sighed. *What a dick.* She turned her back to him and strolled out of the office. She'd found a snack room with a cupboard full of goodies on the other side of the floor when she'd cleared it. Her stomach growled at the thought of food.

Chomping on a bag of chips, she turned the radio back on. Was Butler listening for something from her?

She changed the channel back to the active one she'd first found. Still some traffic about Medical Lake. Sounded like they'd caught a significant horde and were busy clearing it out.

"Base to all units. Base to all units. Zulu activity increasing in Spokane. All units directed to evacuate from Spokane and back to base. Do not engage. Repeat. Return to base and do not engage."

What the hell?

An Apache helicopter flew overhead, heading back to base. Jen ran back to the office. Morgan looked up at her as she entered. Something on her face got his attention.

"What's wrong?" he asked.

Sunrays shot like laser beams across the room. Jen peeked through the blinds and onto the street below. It was flooded with zombies, both human and the occasional canine. They looked like ants swarming a dropped ice cream cone on a summer's day.

Jen's heart raced. *Where the hell'd they all come from? And so fast?*

The zombies froze. Jen blinked her eyes. *Did that just happen?*

The radio squawked. "Base to all military units. Stay on this channel. Base to Jen. Switch to channel thirty-two."

"What the hell's your boss up to, now?" She turned to channel thirty-two and keyed the mic. "Butler. You there?"

"Have you looked onto the street lately?" Butler sounded proud of himself.

"Bunch of zombies. Same shit, different day."

"Oh, I think there's some different shit today," Butler said. "Leader One, disperse your troops to search the buildings for Jen Reed. You and your drones have explicit orders to kill, but not infect her. You also have explicit orders to deliver Dr. Morgan safely to me. If any of your drones fail, you will be punished."

Jen chewed the edge of her lip. *Is this shit for real?*

The zombies parted a block away, and a single figure, wearing a plastic helmet and a uniform, walked through them.

"So you've got a leader looking for us? Good luck with that."

The uniformed figure stopped, and the zombies split into groups and poured into buildings.

Butler laughed. "I've got the numbers. They'll find you. And I've been thinking that I'll let the drones capture you and hold you for the leader to kill."

There's something more here. Something he's dying to tell me. "I'll bite. What's the big surprise?"

Butler chuckled. "I guess the leader's not close enough to make out well. But when you do meet face-to-face, why don't you give my regards to Corporal Grant?"

29

J en squinted and tried to make out features of the lone figure, but he disappeared into the financial building across the street. *Could be Grant. Could be a hundred other guys from the base.*

"I guess you're screwed," Morgan said.

Jen blinked. Grant or not, she was in the shit.

She raced to the stairway door and pressed her ear against it. Dozens of footsteps echoed from below. She pushed on her blockade. It'd keep dozens back, but they'd just call for reinforcements and get through, anyhow.

She hiked her rifle on her shoulder and pulled Morgan from the chair.

"There's no place to run," he said.

She pushed him in front of her. "Move. Down the hall."

He shrugged and lumbered down the hallway and around the corner. She stopped him at a door with a sign that read "Roof Access."

Morgan laughed. "This is your plan? What are you going to do, jump?"

She pulled his cuffed hands up, stretching the ligaments

in his shoulders. He cried out. "Maybe I'm going up there to push you off. Ever think of that?"

Pulling the door open, she shoved him through. *Truth is, I have no idea what I'm doing. But one thing I've learned in the last month is there are always ways out if you look for them.*

They reached the roof and the door slammed shut behind them. "Sit," she said.

Morgan sat, cross-legged, watching her with interest, but keeping his mouth shut.

Jen ran to the far corner. No roofs close enough to jump onto. She checked out each corner in turn, with the same result.

I really screwed this one up. Should've made sure I had a escape route when I chose the building. Mark would've done that.

Movement caught her attention. The figure in uniform walked, head down, across the roof of the financial building. It took slow, purposeful steps, and stopped opposite from Jen. She walked to the edge of the roof to get a better look. It lifted its head.

Grant.

Grant's yellow eyes bore into hers. Without a movement or a word from him, the other buildings emptied and the zombies dashed into hers.

Jen unslung the rifle from her shoulder and aimed it at Grant. He stood unmoving, but quivered in her sights as she fought to control her breathing.

It's not Grant anymore. It's Butler's tool.

Banging came from the door. *Not much time.* She dropped to a knee, propping an elbow on a kneecap to steady herself. She took a deep breath, aimed, and let out half her breath. Faces flashed through her mind: her father, Doc, Chris. Tears welled in her eyes. *I'm sorry, Grant.* She squeezed the trigger and the bullet went through Grant's left eye and blew his zombie brains and pieces of the shattered helmet across the rooftop. He wavered for a second, then flopped onto his back, disappearing behind the roof's raised edge.

She swallowed. *All he wanted was to get back to Kodiak to check on his family.*

Zombies in the street stopped in their tracks, then shuffled aimlessly. Many wandered onto the street from her building.

She turned toward Morgan, who sat with his head hung. "Guess you assholes didn't think about someone taking out your leaders," she said. "Pretty easy fix."

Jen keyed the mic. "Uh, Butler. I think your dastardly plan to conquer the world has hit a snag."

The radio remained silent. Jen shoved the mic toward Morgan. "Maybe you better tell him."

She keyed the mic. "Butler, this is Morgan. She shot the leader. All the drones will return to their default behavior."

"What the hell does that mean?" Butler's voice was laced with fury.

"They'll wander around until they spot a meal, or there's some other disturbance," Morgan said.

Jen took the mic. "Not too smart, Butt head. Should've kept your general in the rear, where he was safe."

Morgan's head drooped forward. *Time to press the advantage.* "How about that prisoner swap? Seems like you're out of options."

Come on, Butler. Come on.

"One hour," Butler said. "Hotel. I'll be there."

"Roger Dodger." Jen switched back to the main radio channel to hear the normal chatter. She grinned at Morgan. "Let's listen in for a while."

Something banged against the rooftop door. Jen pulled

her axe. The door rattled with the next blow, and Jen pressed her ear to it. One, maybe two zombies. Better to take them out before they drew a crowd.

Morgan scooted away from the door, his eyes wide.

Jen took several steps backward and laid her rifle on the ground before taking a stance next to the door. Grasping the handle, she took a deep breath. *One, two, three.*

She swung the door open and four zombies fell onto the roof. She glanced inside and confirmed none remained, so she slammed the door shut and spun to face the threat.

A middle-aged man in a business suit charged her. She swung, but missed his head, the axe biting into his neck and knocking him down.

Two other zombies approached from opposite sides. She feinted at one, using the momentum to bury the axe into the bridge of the other zombie's nose. It stumbled backward, but didn't fall.

Shit.

Morgan screamed. Jen glanced his way. The fourth zombie shambled toward him as he slid his ass across the rooftop.

The businessman had regained his feet and raced toward her, the other two zombies coming at her again from the sides.

On pure instinct, she swung and caught the businessman in the temple at the same time she ducked and spun, causing one of her attackers to rush by and slam into the other one.

The businessman fell to the ground and lay still. The other two attempted to untangle their limbs, but Jen made quick work of them.

Morgan's screams went up an octave. The last zombie

had him by the leg and pulled him toward his snapping jaws.

Jen dashed toward the zombie and tackled it just as it lifted Morgan's leg to its mouth. Jen lost her grip on the axe and it skittered away. She jumped to her feet and scrambled for it as the zombie gave chase a few feet behind. Jen leapt for the axe, rolled, and swung it upward, catching the zombie on the chin and ruining its jaw.

It grasped her leg and went for the meal. Jen kicked at it with her other leg, loosening its grip. Jumping to her feet, she swung and split the zombie's forehead. It flopped to the ground.

Panting, Jen stumbled to Morgan, who lay on his side facing away from her.

"I took care of it," she said. "Now you and I need to get ready for the trade."

Morgan rolled over and glowered at her with yellow eyes.

30

J en kicked Morgan onto his stomach and pulled him up by his cuffed hands. His pant leg rolled up, exposing an oozing bite wound on his ankle. Morgan kicked and twisted, but was no match for her. "You're still a little guy. It's not like the movies where zombies have super strength and shit."

She brought him to the edge of the roof and scoped out the street. A few groups of zombies bunched together and wandered, but most of them had left in search of food.

She pulled him back. "What the hell am I going to to do with you now? Butler will never make the trade."

A pipe ran up the side of the raised rooftop entry, leaving an inch between it and the wall. Jen slammed Morgan into it and removed her belt. She looped it through Morgan's cuffed hands and around the pipe before fastening it tightly.

She stepped back to admire her handiwork. Morgan growled and snapped his jaws, but stayed put. Jen left him and walked down the stairs to the top floor.

The desks she'd piled in front of the stairway door lay

askew like a child's blocks. A single zombie rushed out of the doorway and bore down on her. Its silky blonde hair, missing tufts from its bloody scalp, flew in the breeze.

Jen stepped into its path, brought the axe down, and sent the zombie to its rest. She closed the stairway door and restacked the desks.

In one office, she found a huge purse sitting on a desk lined with pictures of children, old people, and cats. Lots of cats. Jen emptied the purse on the desk. A wallet with an ID of a gray-haired lady with deep dimples fell out. Jen left it all and headed for the roof with the purse in hand.

Morgan still struggled against his bonds, and moaned pitifully. "I need to keep you a secret just long enough to make the trade," Jen said. "Then I don't give a shit if he knows you're dead."

She pulled the upside-down purse over Morgan's head. It covered him down to his chest. Morgan stopped struggling and stood silently.

"I've seen you assholes get quieter in the dark," she said, "but I didn't expect this to work that good."

She tuned the radio to the main military frequency. Chatter erupted from it. "Echo Five to base. Copy we're downtown Spokane. Setting up position as ordered."

Jen looked up and down the street. *There.* A Humvee idled three blocks away.

She wandered back to Morgan. "Looks like your boss thinks he's smart."

More voices on the radio reported positions. *Did he bring his whole army?*

All of the signals were strong. They were all around her. Butler had laid a trap.

The distant sound of rotors came from the west. Jen stood on the eastern side of the raised rooftop entry and watched a dot in the distance. She changed the channel back to thirty-two.

"Command One to Jen. Do you read?"

"Copy," she said.

"Approaching the hotel rooftop with your friends. ETA three minutes."

Jen checked her weapons' loads and the rooftop door. *Secure.*

She scanned the neighboring rooftops for leaders or snipers, but found no sign of either.

The soft *thup thup* of the rotors got louder as the helicopter grew in size. It approached the hotel building.

Jen keyed her mic. "Two buildings to your right."

She stepped out from cover and waved at the Blackhawk. It changed course and landed on the far side of the roof. Only the pilot was visible. He hit some switches and the rotors slowed. Jen took cover behind Morgan and aimed at the helicopter's door as it slid open.

Butler climbed out, his pistol to the head of a bound and gagged Mark, the visible parts of his face crimson. Zeke jumped down next to them, his legs tied as well as his hands.

Not so dumb. Zeke could probably kick the shit out of him with his hands tied.

"No bullshit," she called out. "I'll put a bullet in his head if I even think you're going to pull something."

Butler pushed Mark forward and Zeke hopped next to him. "I don't need tricks. Once I get Morgan back, he'll work up another helmet. I've got plenty of leaders to send out and I'll have ten thousand zombies out here tracking you down."

Jen pressed the pistol barrel into Morgan's head. He stirred. She let off on the pressure. "Then maybe I should just take Morgan out now."

Butler shrugged, then licked his lips. *Son of a bitch wants me to think he doesn't give a shit, but he can't hide it.*

"You could do that," he said. "But I'm betting you won't. Your odds of escaping suck, but at least you have a chance if you make the exchange."

And your mad scientist is useless to you now.

Jen cut Morgan's zip ties, praying that he didn't start grabbing at her. "Untie them and we'll send them over at the same time."

A knife appeared in Butler's hand. "Back up to me," he said to Zeke. Zeke hopped backward and Butler leaned down and sawed through the ropes around his ankles, but kept his pistol pressed into Mark's back. "Don't try shit or your buddy here dies."

He cut Zeke's wrists loose and the ninja removed his gag. Butler pointed the knife to a spot twenty feet to his side. "Move your ass."

Zeke sauntered over to the spot and turned back, rubbing his wrists. *Of all of us up here, he's got the biggest balls.*

Butler freed Mark and shoved him forward. "Let's get this done."

Jen guided Morgan forward while Mark and Zeke walked toward her.

"Not you, girl." Butler pointed his pistol at Mark. "Just the hostages."

Shit. What if Morgan just stands there? She released Morgan's arm and backed away. Mark and Zeke continued toward her, but Morgan didn't move.

"What's wrong with him?" Butler asked. "Morgan?"

"I had to sedate him," Jen said. "He was freaking out and attracting zombie attention, so I found some pills and gave him a couple."

Butler stepped forward, waving his gun at her. "All of you get back."

Jen nodded at Mark and Zeke, and they moved back to the rooftop door.

Butler approached Morgan. "Come on, Morgan. Our ride's waiting."

He pulled the purse off Morgan's head and froze. Jen couldn't see Morgan's face, but Butler's bug-eyed expression told her all she needed to know.

Mark and Zeke looked at her, their eyes questioning. She shrugged. "Morgan got bit."

Morgan sprung at Butler, who pushed him to the side.

Jen knelt into a firing position and put a round in Butler's midsection. He stumbled backward, his arms splayed.

The helicopter started up. Jen aimed at the pilot through the glass. "Shut it down," she yelled.

The pilot ignored her and the rotors sped up. She moved closer. "Last chance," she yelled.

A hand grabbed hers and pulled upward, the pistol aiming to the sky. "No," Mark said. "We don't kill soldiers that aren't trying to kill us."

"Butler," Jen said. Mark released her. She aimed her pistol back at Butler. He teetered on the edge of the roof, a red stain spreading over his shirt. Morgan crept toward him like a leopard stalking its prey.

"This is for Grant, you asshole." Jen squeezed the trigger and the gun fired just as Morgan leapt at Butler. The bullet slammed into Butler's chest and he tumbled off the roof. Morgan couldn't stop his leap and disappeared over the side.

The Blackhawk hovered over the hotel as Jen rushed to where Butler and Morgan had fallen. Butler's body lay across the crumpled roof of a car, his head hanging over the side. Morgan lay unmoving on the sidewalk, a dark red splat on the pavement around his head.

Mark grabbed her arm. "We've got to go. I don't know what's going on, but that damn helicopter is tracking us."

Jen handed Mark her rifle. "You're a better shot than me. I might actually shoot the pilot."

Mark jacked a round into the chamber, took aim, and fired at the helicopter. A crack appeared in the windshield a foot from the pilot. The helicopter spun and raced back in the direction of base.

Zeke ran up, Jen's radio in his hand. "Listen to this."

Broken chatter came from the radio, mostly units reporting readiness and being in position. A voice broke through. "This is Hotel Three to all units. Command One is down. I repeat, Command One is down and unrecoverable. His last orders are to implement Operation Smoke Out. I repeat. All ground and air units are to implement Operation Smoke Out immediately."

Crackles and more broken voices came over the air before one broke through. "Echo Two to Echo teams, let's go get the bastards that killed the colonel."

Mark frowned. "We're in the shit."

Jen let out a mirthless chuckle. "I think we're permanent residents."

"Guys," Zeke said. "Come here."

Jen turned to Zeke, who stood at the roof's edge looking down. "What?"

Zeke pointed to the sidewalk. "I see Morgan, but where's Butler?"

Jen squinted at the empty indent in the car's roof. "Are you shitting me?"

31

J en looked at Mark. "That son of a bitch didn't damage his head." She stalked toward the door.

Mark grabbed her arm. "What the hell are you doing?"

"Let me go. I'm going to finish what I started."

Mark released her. "We've got bigger things to worry about than your revenge against Butler."

She poked him in the chest. "You didn't have to shoot Grant."

Zeke's mouth dropped open. "You shot Grant? Did you kill him?"

Jen squeezed her eyes shut and pressed the heels of her hands into her temples. "No. I mean, yes. But really Butler did." She opened her eyes and tears raced down her face. "They made him a leader and sent him after me. There were thousands of drones in this building, and Grant stood over there." She pointed at the roof across the road, Grant's body out of sight behind the raised edge. "Only way I could stop them was to take Grant out."

Mark's voice softened. "We didn't know that, but it

doesn't change anything. We need to get to Atlanta and brief Dr. Cartwright on the latest mutations."

"He's right," Zeke said. "If we destroy the zombies, that'll mean Butler, too."

Jen bit her lip. *It's not like Butler's downstairs waiting for me.* "OK. Let's get to the Humvee."

Mark put up a hand. "Wait." He tilted his head, then ran to the roof's edge. He ducked and clambered back to them.

"Ground troops coming down the road. Humvees, armored carriers, and ground pounders. Looks to be five, six hundred."

"They know where we are." Jen clasped the door handle. "Come on."

Mark ran to her, but Zeke stood, overlooking the street. "You're gonna want to see this."

Jen joined Zeke and her legs almost gave out. Everywhere for two square blocks, the street and sidewalk had filled with zombies.

"How they hell did that happen so fast?" Mark asked.

Jen pointed below. The zombies pushed into their building. "They know we're here, too. Are these damn things evolving again? It's like they don't need Butler pulling the strings anymore."

"Where do we go?" Zeke asked.

Mark raced to the door and opened it. "They're coming up. There's a ton of them."

Nowhere to jump. Can't fight them. And no way down while they're on the stairs.

Jen snapped her fingers. "Why didn't I think of it before? Follow me."

She ran down the stairs to the sixth floor with Zeke and Mark on her heels and dashed into the hallway, stopping at the elevator doors. She tried to pull them apart. Damn doors didn't move. "Help."

Mark and Zeke stepped up and together the three of them pulled the doors open a few feet.

Jen turned on her flashlight and shined it down the shaft. The top of the elevator sat three floors below.

"You're not thinking what I think you're thinking, are you?" Mark asked.

Zeke stood in the doorway, rocked his arms a few times, and leapt into the shaft, grabbing the cable. Like a natural, he shimmied his way down to the car.

"OK, now you're just showing off," Jen said.

A crash in the stairway nearly stopped her heart. She stepped inside the elevator doors, balancing on the narrow ledge. "Unless you have a better idea, it's now or never."

Mark slid in next to her and shined his light on the cable. "You first. When you get to the elevator car, you can give me light."

Jen nodded. She tried to follow Zeke's example the best she could and leapt into the murky shaft.

She lost sight of the cable mid-jump and hit it with her chest. Wrapping her arms around it, she slid down the braided line.

Coming in too fast.

Her arms grew hot from the friction. Wrapping her legs around the cable, she squeezed. She still dropped, but at a slower pace.

Zeke stood on the car and reached out to her. She hopped down next to Zeke and wobbled, her arms wind-milling. He grabbed her shirt and pulled her back.

"Isn't that a kick in the ass?" he said.

"Not exactly the phrase I'd use."

She whipped out her flashlight and pointed the beam at

Mark. Tromping footsteps thudded through the walls. Vibrations from the swarming zombies made their way up through her shoes. *There's got to be a thousand in this building alone and they'll be on Mark's floor at any minute.*

Mark jumped and caught the cable like it was a move he'd practiced. He slid down, stepping onto the car with a light step.

"You made that look easy," Jen whispered.

He shrugged. "Army. Rappelling."

Zeke lifted a small door in the top of the car. "Let's get out of sight." He dropped into the car and Jen landed next to him. Mark closed the door as he joined them.

Jen shined her light on Zeke. "You look different."

Zeke turned around in the light. "Only thing different is I don't have my katana. I feel naked."

"That's it," she said. She pulled her pistol and axe. "Which one do you want? Mark has my rifle."

Zeke took the axe and balanced it in his hand, then lay it down and picked up the pistol. "I'm too used to the katana as my melee weapon. I'll take the pistol."

An explosion from below shook the car.

"What the hell?" Mark said.

Jen's pulse raced. "Don't tell me they're sending artillery again."

Another explosion, this one closer, nearly knocked her to her knees.

Mark sat on the floor. "We can't leave the elevator until the zombies are gone, and you're more likely to get hurt if you fall. So you might as well take a seat."

Jen grumbled, but lowered herself to the floor. "I wonder if those ground troops have engaged the horde."

Zeke pointed to her belt. "What about your radio?"

Jen pulled the radio out. She turned the volume down before turning it on.

"Echo Four to Control. Multiple Zulu units encountered. Repeat. These things are organized They're attacking in a tactical manner."

"Control to Hotel Two. Request assistance at Echo Two's location."

"Roger Base. This is Hotel Two. I have enough fuel and ammo to make one more run then need to return for resupply."

"Roger. All units, this is base. Our ground forces have met extreme resistance. Thousands of Zulus are attacking. Our units are defeating them and have nearly captured Second Avenue."

"Sounds like they're right outside this building," Jen said. "Artillery should slacken off now, shouldn't it?"

Mark nodded and put his head against the elevator doors. "Still a bunch of zombies running around out there."

The radio chatter increased. They announced that the zombies had been routed. "Clear the building and find the civilians."

"Command One to all units. Those civilians are important to national security. Find them and get them back here safely."

Mark raised an eyebrow. "Who's that?"

"One way to find out," Jen said. Mark's eyes widened and he tried to grab the radio from her, but she pulled it away.

"Command One, this is the civilians. Who am I talking to?"

"Civilian radio operator, switch to channel thirty-two."

Jen adjusted the radio. "This is Jen Reed. Who's this?"

"Miss Reed, this is General Lewis. I arrived on base a

short while ago to relieve Colonel Butler of his command. What's your location?"

"Not so fast. Who sent you?"

"Dr. Cartwright."

Jen looked at Mark. He shrugged. "Sorry, General. We've been lied to enough that we're not taking any chances."

"Jen, Dr. Cartwright sent me. Now give me your location. We have teams in your area that can get you back safely."

"I'm afraid you'll have to give me more than that, General."

The radio remained silent. Jen keyed the mic. "General?"

"Jen, this is Sergeant Howell."

Mark's eyes went wide. "Well, what do you know?"

Jen held a hand up. "Go ahead."

"General Lewis is the real deal. We need you to come in."

"Damn," Zeke said. "Just when things are heating up."

Jen keyed the mic. "I still haven't heard the magic phrase."

"I'll eat a bug if I'm lying," said Howell.

Gunshots came from below. Men shouted. The staccato sound of automatic weapons came from just outside the elevator doors.

Jen looked at Zeke and he said, "Them's the code words."

Mark frowned. "It's the right thing to say, but I'm still hesitant. What if he's under duress?"

"Cartwright mentioned the other day that she had a meeting with General Lewis," Jen said.

"Command One to Miss Reed. Did you copy?"

Mark put his hands up. *He's letting me make the decision.* She keyed the mic. "General, we're hidden in the same building Colonel Butler landed on."

"Roger that. Hold tight. A unit is clearing that building now. I'll contact you when it's safe."

Twenty minutes later, footsteps tromped up and down the hall. Voices murmured.

"Command One to Jen Reed. Your building is secure. What's your location?"

Here goes nothing. "Elevator. Third floor."

She switched the radio back to the default channel just in time to hear Lewis. "Command One to Echo Three."

"Echo Three here."

"Roger, Echo Three. The package is in the elevator, third floor."

"Copy."

Someone banged on the door and yelled, "This is Echo Three. We're opening the doors. The building is clear, so put down your weapons."

Mark nodded and laid his gun on the floor. "Don't want anyone to accidentally get shot."

Jen placed her axe in her belt, and Zeke put his gun down.

The door opened and light streamed in. Jen squinted and shaded her eyes. "You our ride?"

A soldier offered her a hand and she took it. He pulled her to his feet. "Sergeant Washington, ma'am."

Another soldier had a radio to his lips. "Echo Three to Command One. We have the civilians and all look healthy."

"Roger, Echo Three. Get them back here."

The soldier helped Mark and Zeke up. "Let's go."

Mark hesitated. "If it's all the same to you, I'd like to keep my weapon."

"Me, too," Zeke said.

The soldier nodded. "Agreed. Get 'em and follow us."

"Hotel One to all units. Reports of Zulu buildup six blocks north of your location. Prepare to advance and engage."

"Base to all units. Aerial recon reports a horde of one thousand Zulus in sector twenty-three. All units are to advance to that location and engage."

A smattering of responses followed, then the channel went silent.

Sergeant Washington jogged to the stairs with two of his men. Zombie bodies and parts lay strewn over the hallway. Jen avoided what she could and tread carefully over what she couldn't.

They reached the double glass doors and walked outside. Jen nearly gagged and covered her nose and mouth. More bodies littered the landscaping and the streets, and flies hovered over the corpses.

The rumbling of Humvees and APCs echoed between the buildings as they raced north. An Apache zipped by in the same direction.

"Looks like a battle brewing," Jen said.

Washington looked at one of his corporals. "Shit. And we're gonna miss it."

Jen gave him a smile. "You don't have to."

32

Sergeant Washington shook his head. "No motherfucking way. I have my orders. And from a damn general."

"Your buddies need you," Mark said. "I was army. I know how that feels. We'll just drive the Humvee we took back to the base and you can join the battle."

The corporal stepped next to Sergeant Washington. "Come on, Wash. The way back's clear. We all just came that way. If any of my friends get wasted out there, I won't be able to handle it if I didn't at least try to help."

Another corporal nodded. "Same here, Wash. Besides, what's this general know? Probably been a pencil pusher his whole career."

Sergeant Washington glared at Jen from under a lowered brow. "We have our orders."

"You're absolutely right, Sergeant." Mark pointed to the Humvee Jen had escaped in the night before. "But we should drive this back out. You can cover our rear. It's safer."

"Safer how?"

"If one of the vehicles goes Tango Uniform, then we have another. It also gives us two mounted M60s instead of one."

Washington scratched his neck. "Then one of my crew will drive it."

"Not a good idea," Mark said. "You need your team to stay as one cohesive unit. I can drive it. Spent a lot of time doing that a few years back in the sandbox."

"And if you take off on us, my ass is grass."

Mark stuck out his hand. "From one soldier to another, you have my word we won't."

Washington squinted. "I will kick your ass if you fuck me over."

"I'd expect nothing less."

"All right," Washington said. "Mount up, everyone."

The radio came to life.

"Echo Fourteen to Control. Request immediate assistance in sector twenty-three. We underestimated the enemy strength and are trapped between hordes."

Washington put his hand up. "Wait a second."

"Control to Hotel One. Proceed to sector twenty-three and relay sitrep."

"Hotel One to Control. Already at location. Situation is grim. Four hordes of two thousand Zulus and up are attacking sector twenty-three from different directions. Multiple friendly units are engaging, but have no way to retreat."

"Roger. All units attack sector twenty-three from the south. Make a hole and get those units free."

Mark pounded his fist on the Humvee's hood. "They're throwing everything they have at them. They could lose all of their ground forces."

"It almost sounds like a trap," Zeke said.

Jen's eyes went wide. "Shit. I think you're right." She

jumped into the Humvee and keyed the mic. "Control, order a full retreat."

"What the hell are you doing?" Washington ran to Jen. "Are you crazy, woman?"

"Control to unauthorized transmission. Stand down. You're interfering with national security operations."

"No," Jen yelled into the mic. "The buildup of zombies is a trap."

"Echo Two to Control. We're attacking the enemy's southern flank, but there's a massive movement on our flank. Large numbers of combatants are pouring out of an underground garage and attacking our rear."

"Command One to all ground units. Retreat. I say again. Retreat to highway. All air units provide cover."

Zeke tilted his head. "Something coming."

Jen strained to listen and picked up the first rumblings of engines. Several Humvees and APCs zoomed past them.

"Let's get the fuck out of here," Washington yelled. "You people head for the highway and stay with our units until we get there. We'll cover your asses."

Mark jumped into the driver's seat and started the vehicle. Zeke hopped into the back, behind Jen's seat. Mark crushed the accelerator. "Dammit. Wish we had the acceleration of the truck right now."

They turned onto South Division Street and headed for the highway. Washington's crew were a hundred feet behind.

"If those other units passed us that fast," Jen said, "the horde can't be far behind."

Washington's Humvee drove up their ass. Jen glanced back, and Washington waved at them to go faster. Movement farther back caught her eye. "Oh my God."

A tidal wave of zombies chased them from a few blocks

back. The mass of silent monsters ran at full tilt, filling the street, sidewalks, everything.

Mark had slowed to weave around stalled cars. "No slowing down for anything," he said. The engine growled and he sped up.

"The on-ramp's there." Jen pointed ahead.

Mark screeched onto the ramp. The surviving Humvees and APCs had parked in the middle of the road. Soldiers lined the guard rail, their guns aimed to the north.

Mark pulled beside an APC and stopped. They climbed out of the Humvee and grouped at the guard rail.

Washington pulled up next to them. "Get back in your vehicle and stay with us. We're going back to base."

A lieutenant approached them. "Sergeant, I just spoke with Command One on an alternate channel. The civilians are to stay here until this whole convoy goes back to base."

"Yes, sir," Washington said. "Where do you want us to set up?"

"Take your unit to our right flank. There's indication of enemy forces gathering in that direction."

"But, sir, we're supposed to stay with the civilians."

"We'll take over that responsibility." The lieutenant banged a fist against the side of the Humvee. "Now go."

Without another word, Washington's crew sped off to the other end of the line.

The lieutenant pointed at Mark. "You people stay here until and unless you hear different from me."

"Yes, Lieutenant," Mark said. The lieutenant strode off.

"Hotel Two to all units. Prepare to engage."

Jen put a hand out to Zeke. "Give me the rifle."

He handed it over. "What am I going to use?"

Jen pointed at the M60 atop their Humvee. Zeke's mouth dropped. "Jen, I love you." He scampered off to the vehicle.

Jen and Mark knelt behind the guard rail and aimed north. An Apache swooped overhead and back toward base.

Rumbling came from between the buildings in the distance. It reminded Jen of the sounds in a bowling alley.

Waves of undead pulsed down the road four blocks away. Jen's heart thudded. She looked from the thousands in the horde to the hundreds of defenders on the highway. *This is going to be a slaughter.*

Dozens of radios were on, the voices echoing across them. "Echo One to Alpha Two. Dial in to sector twelve and open fire."

A deafening boom, like a roll of thunder, came from somewhere in the distance behind Jen. The horde saw their prey. They surged forward, and a whistling came from overhead. The city exploded, the concussion knocking Jen onto her ass.

She crawled to her knees and slapped her hands over her ears. Oranges, yellows, and reds burned into her retinas. Black smoke rose and the blistering artillery attacks seemed to go on forever.

Until it didn't. Buildings were flattened and others stood in ruins, their remains ablaze. Thick black smoke curled into the sky.

Jen glanced back. Zeke raised his hands in victory, yelling something she couldn't hear. He stopped, his eyes widening, and pointed into the city. Jen turned back around. The black smoke had parted and thousands more figures poured though it and toward the highway.

Soldiers fired. Jen hadn't heard an order, but fired anyway. The mounted .50 cal behind her boomed as it tore into the wave of undead.

But still the horde gained ground. *We'd need double or triple our number to keep them back.*

A jet fighter streaked low over the city, dropping canisters over the horde. They broke open and burst into hellfire as they spread across the landscape.

Mark yelled into her ear. "Napalm. It'll stop them."

Jen shook her head. She remembered the zombies at Point Wallace. They caught on fire, sure, but it didn't stop them.

As if to prove her case, the fires died down, but the flaming figures pressed forward. She glanced at Mark and his face held sheer terror.

Voices came over the radio, but she couldn't make them out. She dialed the radio to maximum volume and pressed it to her ear.

"All units. Take cover. Bombers coming in close."

Far above, the outline of several B52s swept across the sky like ghosts. Again the whistling sound seemed all around her.

She grabbed Mark's arm and he looked at her. Pulling him toward the ground, she pointed upward. He got the message and flattened next to her on the asphalt. She covered her ears just before the ground shook.

A flash of heat hit her side and she thought she'd burst into flame. Her teeth rattled as bomb after bomb exploded several hundred yards away. When the explosions stopped twenty minutes later, Jen used the rail to pull herself to her feet.

For a mile in front of her, the ground was flattened. Buildings burned and black smoke roiled into the sky, blotting out the sun. Mark stood next to her. "Looks like we got them."

Jen nodded. "What I don't get is why they charged right at us."

"What do you mean?"

"If they're getting smarter leaders," she said, "then you'd think they'd be a bit more tactical than just running their drones into a meat grinder."

Mark shrugged. "They've got millions more. Guess they can sacrifice a few thousand."

Shouting came from farther down the line. Jen leaned over the rail to look, but couldn't see a thing.

"Jen. Mark."

Jen spun around. Zeke stood on the Humvee's hood, waving wildly. "They're coming up the highway."

Jen climbed up beside him and shielded her eyes. About a mile past the last military vehicle, an undulating mass pushed forward. "Shit. There's got to be ten thousand of them."

She caught movement from the corner of her eye and turned. A wave of zombies roared up the highway embankment behind the vehicles. They were outflanked.

33

J en fired to the rear. "Behind us!"

The soldiers reacted to the scores of zombies leaping over the railing and streaking toward them.

Zeke jumped into the gunner position and let off three-round bursts from the M60. One zombie went down, its head a stump on its shoulders, and another fell to the side as its knees were blown out.

"Echo Two to Alpha One. Concentrate fire twenty yards south of our position and fire for effect."

Mark pulled Jen behind a Humvee. "This is going to be harsh."

Jen lay beneath the Humvee, firing at the advancing undead. "If we don't take these assholes out quick, the ones running up the highway will be on us."

Distant thunder boomed. When she heard the whistling, Jen plugged her fingers in her ears.

The artillery rounds hit the embankment on the other side, throwing chunks of earth and pieces of zombies into the air. The odor of burnt dead flesh became overpowering.

Four volleys and the artillery ended. Jen pulled herself

to her feet. Mark straightened next to her, and Zeke popped his head up in the Humvee's gunner position.

"Something's definitely pulling strings," Jen said. "This is all too coordinated."

The radio crackled. "Echo Seven to Control. Advancing horde is one hundred yards to engagement."

"Control to all units. Return to base. I say again. Return to base."

The Humvees were loaded and took off one-by-one. Jen looked around for Washington and his crew. She elbowed Mark. "Where's Washington?"

Mark pointed down the road. "There."

Washington and two of his crew sprinted up the highway toward them, the tidal wave of undead at their heels.

Jen jumped into the driver's seat and started the Humvee. Mark slid in next to her. "What the hell are you doing?"

Zeke called down. "There are still some of those flanking zombies. They're going to cut those soldiers off."

"Like hell." Jen threw the vehicle into gear and goosed the gas pedal. The three soldiers still ran, but had also noticed the flanking zombies. They shot at them as their paths came closer.

The chatter of the M60 cut through the air and mixed with Zeke's cries of delight as he cut down zombie after zombie.

Jen swung the Humvee to the side where the flankers were and knocked several over while running over even more. She brought the Humvee in an arc while Mark threw the back door open. Washington threw one of his men in and dove in behind him. A zombie grabbed the third soldier's shirt collar, yanking him back into the horde.

Jen gunned the accelerator while Zeke's M60 chattered away and Washington pulled the door shut. The Humvee pulled away from the horde and down the highway toward the base.

"Shit," Washington said. "You came back for us."

The corporal clapped Jen on the shoulder. "You guys are lifesavers. We owe you."

"Sorry about the other two," Jen said.

Washington's head bowed. "Mitchell and Johnson. Both good soldiers."

The other vehicles were long gone, but the road was clear and the horde fell back into the distance.

Zeke called down. "We've got a problem. Look off to the right."

Jen craned her neck and took in the northern part of the city. Fires still burned to their rear, but the rest remained untouched.

She steered the Humvee farther to the right to get a better view and her breath hitched. Zombies poured out from between every damn building in sight. "Holy shit."

Mark's eyes stayed on the extended horde. "There's not just ten thousand of those fuckers out there. There's got to be a million or more."

Washington leaned forward. "Hand me the mic and keep the pedal down."

Jen tossed the mic to the sergeant and he keyed it. "Echo Three to Base. We're bringing up the rear on the retreat and there's a huge horde coming in from the north. Estimated number is in the millions."

"Command One to Echo Three. This is General Lewis. Confirm the number."

"Yes, sir. The number is estimated to be in the millions, and they're swarming south."

"Roger. Command One to all air units. Proceed to the north and engage the enemy. Alpha One coordinate artillery with Alpha Two and additional air units from Minot and Grand Forks. Put up a wall of death those bastards can't pass."

"Alpha One acknowledges."

The highway curved south and the horde was soon out of sight.

"Command One to Echo Three. Do you have the location of the civilians?"

"Roger, Command One. They're with this unit. All three accounted for and unharmed."

"Bring them to me as soon as you arrive."

"Yes, sir."

THEY ARRIVED at the main gate ten minutes later. While the wall looked foreboding, Jen imagined a million zombies attacking it at once and could think of no scenario in which it kept them out.

She pulled the vehicle through the gate. "I suppose the general's at Headquarters."

"Good guess," Washington said.

Humvees sped by, and fully armed troops ran in formation toward the front gate. A jet launched from the flight line, fire roaring from its engines.

Jen parked in front of Headquarters a few minutes later. A short, stocky soldier with close-cropped salt-and-pepper hair marched out, followed by a trio of NCOs and Sergeant Howell. The older soldier had two stars sewn in his lapel.

Washington and his crewman snapped to attention and saluted. "Echo Three reporting mission accomplished, sir."

General Lewis popped a salute back and stopped in

front of Jen. "Dr. Cartwright seems to think you're essential to the war effort."

"I'm not sure about that," Jen said. "She sent me a two-star general. If I was that important, wouldn't she have sent someone with a five star rating instead of two?"

Lewis stared at her while the NCOs behind him turned various shades of red. All except Howell, who struggled to keep a straight face. "Cartwright warned me about you. She was spot-on. Follow me." He flashed a grin, then turned and marched into the building. Jen winked at Mark as they followed the general.

The general led them to the conference room. One of the NCOs turned on the video conference system. "Guess it wasn't too screwed up if they got it fixed already," Zeke said.

The screen displayed Cartwright with dark circles under her eyes. A tired smile tugged at the corners of her mouth. "Jen."

A soldier burst into the room. "General, you're needed in the war room."

"Sergeant Howell, you stay with the civilians. The rest of you come with me." Lewis hurried out of the room, the NCOs trailing in his wake.

Cartwright put a hand up. "I'm sure you have a lot to tell me, but that can wait till you get here. I understand there's a major attack in progress, and with Colonel Butler dead, the urgency is getting you out of there and not on your report. General Lewis has ordered your plane to be refueled and ready for immediate takeoff. I also asked the general's permission for Specialist Grant to accompany you to Atlanta."

Jen swallowed. "Butler killed Grant and turned him into a leader. He sent him after me. Grant controlled thousands of drones, so I had to kill him. Once he died, the drones went back to wandering around."

Cartwright's face softened. "I'm sorry about Grant." She straightened. "But you must leave immediately. That includes you, Sergeant Howell."

"But I could be useful here," Howell said.

"I have more use for you here, Sergeant," Cartwright said. "You will return immediately."

Howell nodded, but remained silent.

Mark cleared his throat. "I'm not going yet."

"What?" Jen said. "What about your family?"

Mark shrugged. "All indications are that things are fine in Biloxi. Would that be right, Doctor?"

Cartwright frowned, but nodded.

"My other family needs me here," Mark said. "You saw what's out there."

Zeke stood. "I'm with Mark. This is where the battle is. Not back east."

Jen sighed. "I'm all for pitching in for God and country and all that bullshit, but what difference can we make? At best, we're three more guns."

"Recon," Mark said. "We can take the plane up. Butler diverted all the recon to the city the past few days and they're now all involved in the northern attack. What if there are more coming from the rear?"

"I could have you arrested and transported here," Cartwright said. "And it would take an additional aircraft out of service." She steepled her fingers. "How about a compromise?"

"I'm listening," Mark said.

"You use your plane to scout until you've covered the rear directions fifty miles out," Cartwright said. "Once you've completed that, you fly directly to Grand Forks Air Force

Base in North Dakota, where I have a military transport waiting that will bring you here."

Mark rubbed his chin. "Whether we find anything or not, the general will have information he can use to deploy his troops."

"Deal," Jen said. "We're leaving immediately."

Cartwright nodded. "I'll inform General Lewis." The monitor went blank.

They piled into the Humvee and headed for the flight line. "What are they going to do if we find something?" Zeke said.

"Probably divert some air units to try to keep them back," Howell said.

Jen sighed. "If this base falls, it'll open up everything from North Dakota to Colorado. I don't think we can recover from that."

34

Mark started the Cessna and gave Jen the mic. "How about you be my comm?"

Zeke leaned forward from the backseat. "I can do it."

Jen smiled. *Zeke's the best zombie killer on the team, but when you get right down to it, he's still a big kid.*

She handed him the mic. "Why don't you go ahead and ask for permission to take off?"

He took the mic. "But once we're up," Jen said, "we need your eyes on the ground. I can watch my side and still use the mic, but it's not long enough for you back there."

Zeke nodded. "Are we ready?"

Mark grinned. "The radio's yours, big guy."

Zeke keyed the mic. "Attention, Fairchild Tower, this is..." He lowered the mic. "What's our call sign again?"

Jen looked at the paper the airman handed her before she boarded. "Romeo One."

"Oh, right." Zeke brought the mic to his mouth. "Fairchild Tower, this is Romeo One requesting permission to take off, good buddy."

He released the key. "How was that?"

"I think you could've left the 'good buddy' part off," Howell said.

Mark fiddled with the radio dial. "No answer. I forgot about this crappy radio." He glanced back at Zeke. "Try again."

"Fairchild Tower, this is Romeo One requesting permission for takeoff."

"Romeo One, you have permission for takeoff."

Zeke grinned and handed the mic to Jen. "Not bad, huh?"

Mark engaged the throttle. "You could do it for a living."

Mark guided the plane onto the end of the runway and increased the speed. Other aircraft and buildings sped by in a blur and the Cessna lifted into the air, flying over the wall.

Jen pressed against the window. "They're finally working on that gap in the wall."

"Butler had the combat engineers out looking for you instead of finishing their job," Howell said. "He put the whole base in jeopardy."

Mark craned his neck to get a look. "They're moving fast. The wall's as high as the men working on it."

The plane banked to the right and climbed higher. Black smoke hung over the base and as far north as Jen could see. It looked like it cleared farther south, with a layer of big fluffy clouds blocking the sun.

The radio crackled. "Romeo...status...by General Lewis's order."

Jen keyed the mic. "Fairchild Tower, this is Romeo One. Please repeat. You're breaking up."

"Status update...before...Lewis."

"Dammit," Jen said. "This radio's still a piece of shit."

The plane headed due south. Jen watched Medical Lake pass by beneath them. "Looks pretty clear on my side. Zeke?"

"Same here."

Jen tried the radio again. "Romeo One to Fairchild Tower, do you read?"

A loud buzz from the speakers startled her, and she scrambled to lower the volume.

Zeke stretched his arms. "This is kind of boring. I'd rather be down on the ground killing more zombies."

Howell had his face pressed to the window. "I see a couple zombies below. What about your side, Zeke?"

Zeke quieted and peered out his window.

"What's the first waypoint again?" Mark asked.

Jen consulted the paper. "St. John. Forty-five miles south of base."

"Should be just a ways ahead," Mark said. "Keep your eyes peeled for any hordes."

Jen studied the green-and-brown landscape beneath her. "I've got a horde of about fifty heading south, and another couple of onesies and twosies going in different directions."

"I've got less than that," Zeke said. "Maybe twenty in all."

"So far, so good," Howell said. "No major buildups."

Mark pointed ahead at a small town coming up. "Must be St. John."

They flew over it. "Nothing here," Zeke said.

Jen looked at Mark and shook her head. "Same."

"On to Ritzville." Mark banked the plane to the right.

Jen put the mic to her mouth. "Romeo One to Fairchild. Do you read?"

"This is Fairchild Tower. Command One is requesting your sitrep, Romeo One."

"Roger. Have reached St. John with minimal enemy activity. Now proceeding to Ritzville."

"Roger, Romeo One. Be advised to stay clear of our

airspace on your way to Grand Forks. Increased contact with enemy forces in the area has required artillery and air support. Repeat. Stay out of the theater of operations."

"Roger, Fairchild Tower. Romeo One out."

Howell whistled. "There must be a ton of ordnance dropping there."

"Damn," Zeke said. "Where did all those freaking northern zombies come from?"

"Maybe they're from Canada," Mark said. "I don't remember anyone saying what was going on up there."

"Canadian zombies," Jen said. "Great. At least they'll be polite while they're gnawing your face off."

Zeke sat back in his seat. "This is a waste of time. There's nothing out here. They're all coming from up north."

"Keep your eyes on the ground," Mark snapped.

Jen raised an eyebrow at him and he sighed. "Sorry, Zeke. Didn't mean it that way. But what you're doing's important. If we can clear the other directions, they can fully commit troops to the zombies coming from the north."

"And if anything is coming from the south," Jen said, "they need to know now."

A goofy smile spread across Zeke's face. "No worries. You can count on me."

Jen noted ten different small hordes heading northwest. "So far I've seen a total of a few hundred since St. John, but they're all heading northwest, away from the base."

Mark cracked his neck. "Coming up on Ritzville. Let Fairchild know."

"What's our next waypoint?" Jen asked.

"Fort Spokane."

"Romeo One to Fairchild Tower. Do you read?"

The speakers let out a slight crackle and nothing else.

Jen tried again. "Fairchild Tower, this is Romeo One. Do you read?"

A burst of static, then nothing. Jen slapped the dash. "So are they not hearing us, or are we not hearing their reply?"

Mark banked the plane. "Give them the report. Hopefully they'll hear it."

"Romeo One to Fairchild Tower. Be advised we're not hearing you. Our sitrep is once again minimal enemy activity to Ritzville. Now proceeding to last waypoint at Fort Spokane."

The speakers remained silent. Jen slammed the mic into its holder. "Let's just get this shit done and head to Grand Forks."

Mark straightened. "Hey, I think I see something ahead."

Jen leaned against the dash and peered out the window. A shadow spread across the land that reminded her of bees swarming a hive. *Or more like hornets.*

They approached the area. "I see it out this side, too," Zeke said. "What the heck is it?"

"Oh my God," Howell said. "I hope it isn't what I think it is."

Jen looked out her window. "Mark, bring us down."

"How low?"

"As low as it takes to make this out."

The plane's nose dipped and dropped closer to the ground before leveling off. "How about now?" Mark asked.

"Can you circle here?" Jen asked.

"Got it." The plane banked.

No longer a blur flashing by, the mass came into perfect focus. Jen gasped. "Zombies. Millions of them, and they're heading straight for Fairchild."

35

J en snatched the mic from its holder. *Please work.*

"Romeo One to Fairchild Tower. This is an emergency. Do you read?"

Nothing.

"Romeo One to Fairchild Tower. There's a huge horde heading your way from the west. Do you read?"

"They're coming from the southwest, too," Zeke said. "Look."

Jen peered out the window. The darkness flooded the land as far as she could see. "Oh. My. God."

"And those things are running at full tilt," Mark said. He righted the plane and increased the throttle.

"We've got to go back to Fairchild and warn them," Howell said.

Mark nodded. "Heading back at full speed."

Jen brought the mic to her lips. "Romeo One to Fairchild Tower. There are millions of zombies moving quickly to your location from the west and southwest."

She turned to Mark. "They're going to hit the wall at the

break. They only have that thing up to six feet or so. This horde will wash over it."

"And if they haven't heard your transmissions," Mark said, "Fairchild won't have a chance to reinforce that portion of the wall."

Zeke whistled. "It's like they're doing it on purpose."

"What?" Howell asked.

"The attack from the north is drawing all the firepower there while this larger group moves in from behind. Me and my gaming group did the same thing on this crazy map—"

"Romeo One to Fairchild Tower. Do you read?"

A crackle came from the speaker and Jen threw the mic to the floor. "How much longer?"

Mark hunched over the wheel, biting his lower lip. "Look ahead."

Jen peered out the front window. They were only a couple of miles from the base.

Howell looked down. "We're just clearing the leading edge of that horde. There won't be a lot of time once we land."

Mark shook his head. "I don't know what the hell they can do to plug that hole. If they divert the artillery and air units to the southwest, they might keep the horde from breaching the gap, but then the northern approach is open."

"The general's a smart guy," Howell said. "I don't know if it'll matter, but the base is in the best hands available."

The plane slowed and the nose dipped. "I'm not cleared for landing, so I'm going to buzz the tower to get their attention. Then we're going in."

A Blackhawk lifted off from the runway and flew north. Several bombers streaked high overhead.

The Cessna zipped by the tower, causing several of the

air traffic controllers to duck. "I think we have their attention," Mark said.

Mark took the plane in a wide turn then straightened for the runway. He lowered the flaps and decreased speed. The runway came up to meet them and the plane bounced once, twice, then settled.

Emergency vehicles, their lights flashing, sped toward them.

"Don't stop," Jen said. "Get us to our parking spot. We can jump in the truck and get to HQ faster."

Mark pulled up near the pumps and cut the engine. Without waiting for the props to stop, they hopped out of the plane and ran to the truck. A maintenance crew member looked at them curiously. Jen pointed at him. "Get the plane refueled quickly. We're under orders from General Lewis."

The crewman nodded and ran off.

Howell hopped into the driver's seat and started the truck. The others boarded and the tires left rubber on the tarmac as they tore down the road.

A fire truck roared down the runway and stopped at the Cessna. The MP vehicle made a sharp turn and chased the truck.

Heavy vehicle and troop traffic forced Howell to slow and stop for others. The MP truck pulled up behind and they got out, but the traffic cleared and Howell sped off, causing the MPs to scramble back into their truck and give chase.

The truck arrived at HQ with a screech. Howell threw the truck into park. Jen jumped out just as the MP vehicle pulled up.

"Halt," a bearish-looking MP said, his pistol aimed at her. Jen ignored him and ran into the building. The MP chased after her, but Howell tackled him into a wall, knocking the air out of him. Mark disarmed the second MP and followed Jen.

She burst into Lewis's office. Surrounded by soldiers in full combat gear, he looked up from his desk. "Where the hell have you been? We haven't heard from you since Ritzville."

Howell burst in.

Jen leaned on the general's desk, panting. "Radio problems. Huge horde coming from the south and west. Millions of them. The northern attack is a diversion."

"They're heading here at full tilt, sir," Howell said.

Lewis stood. "Divert all air units to the southwest. Keep half the artillery pounding the north and divert the other half to the southwest. And I want a helicopter out there on recon. We need eyes."

The men scattered and Lewis faced the wall, his head down and hands pressed against his back. "Millions, you say?"

"There had to be," Mark said. "We couldn't see the end of them. I think we found the expected surge from Seattle and Portland."

The general sighed. "There's no way we can hold that back."

Jen swallowed. "I don't think so."

The general turned around. "It's time for you to leave. Cartwright needs you. Our only hope is for some kind of cure, and she needs your blood and the information you have."

Zeke scratched his head. "It'd be a great battle. Imagine how many zombies I could take out."

Lewis sat on the edge of his desk. "We all have our role,

and this isn't yours." He cast a steely gaze at Jen. "You go take care of business."

Jen's throat tightened. She nodded.

The MP burst in. "Sorry, General. I'll get them out of here."

"You see that you do." He pointed at the MP. "Escort them back to their aircraft, Code One. Radio the tower on the way and get them cleared for takeoff. Highest priority."

The MP looked at Jen, then back at the general. "Yes, sir."

Howell saluted Lewis. "Honor to serve with you, sir."

The general returned his salute. "Sergeant, your mission is to get these people safe to Atlanta."

"Yes, sir."

HOWELL FOLLOWED THE MP TRUCK, its lights flashing and siren wailing, through the traffic and to the flight line. "Look," Zeke said.

The zombies had reached the gap. No artillery hits sounded in the south. "I don't think they've re-aimed the artillery yet."

An Apache zoomed over them and sprayed gunfire at the zombies climbing over the wall. "It's too damn late," Mark said. "They can keep some back, but can't bomb the horde at the wall without taking the wall out."

Humvees, APCs, and trucks streaked toward the gap. Ground troops rushed in and took cover, then opened fire.

The zombie wave crashed over the wall, overwhelming the forces lined against them. Soldiers continued pouring fire into the mob, but one by one they disappeared under the wall of undead.

Jen pulled up to the plane. The crewman had a rifle and

fired at zombies washing over an APC. "You're fueled up," he said. "Get the hell out of here."

They piled in and Mark started the engine. "We may not have a clear runway. Hang on."

The MP rolled down his window and gestured for them to follow. Mark nodded.

The leading edge of the mob had reached the runway. A zombie here and a zombie there, it wouldn't be another minute before it was flooded with the main body of the attack.

The MP sped ahead, swerving from side to side and knocking zombies out of the way. Mark pushed the throttle forward. Even with the help, it'd be close.

A mass of zombies poured onto the end of the runway. "Shit," Mark said. "They're shortening the damn runway. Hang on."

He pressed the throttle to the max. The MP truck accelerated, knocking zombies aside, clearing a narrow path for the plane.

The plane lifted as the MP truck plowed into a thick wall of undead and came to a stop. Zombies washed over it.

Mark had the wheel pulled back as far as he could. A drop of sweat tracked down his cheek. "Come on. Come on."

The plane shuddered, then soared over the wall.

"We hit something," Mark said, "but we made it. We'll need to do a tower flyby at Grand Forks and have them check our landing gear for damage."

The plane continued climbing. Mark banked it in a wide circle, and Jen pressed her face to the window.

The undead had penetrated halfway into the base. Gunfire erupted everywhere. Squads of soldiers held their ground and were swept over by the horde.

The battle for Fairchild was over in minutes.

36

J en's heart sank. All those brave men gone. *Turned into drones.*

Howell held his head in his hands. "I don't know how we can stop that."

"We should head to Grand Forks," Mark said. "Report what we've seen."

Zeke had his nose pressed to the window. "Wait. Look there." He pointed to the west.

Howell raised himself up and looked past Zeke. "What the hell is that?"

Jen tried to look. "I can't see shit. What is it?"

"I think we found a leader," Mark said. "Going in for a closer look."

He banked the plane and descended to a couple hundred feet. The base was completely overrun and yet there were still miles of zombies outside its walls.

Mark pointed out the windshield. "Look at that, Jen."

She squinted. Ahead in the sea of undead, one stood alone, the horde flowing around it like a river around a boulder. "Can you circle it?"

Mark put the Cessna into a tight turn, and Jen took out a pair of binoculars. Pressing them to her eyes, she adjusted the focus until the figure came into focus. She hissed as she drew in a sharp breath.

"What is it?" Howell asked.

Zeke leaned forward. "I want to see."

"You won't believe it," Jen said.

"Say it," Mark snapped.

"That's Butler."

Butler threw his hands into the air and every zombie froze. "Holy shit," Mark said. "He's controlling them all. Look, even on the base they're all still."

"My God," Howell said.

Jen peered down at Butler, whose head moved to follow the plane with his yellow eyes. "Let's get the hell out of here and report."

"Agreed," Howell said. "The sooner the better."

Jen pressed both middle fingers against the window. *You'll see me again, you son of a bitch, and then I'll finish the job.*

CONTINUE THE JOURNEY

Get the next book in the Zombie Uprising Series at
http://smarturl.it/TheHybridNovel

AUTHOR'S NOTES

So the plot thickens in the Zombie Uprising world. If you liked The Citadel, *please leave a review on Amazon.* This will help the book reach more people who like the kind of stories you and I do.

I had someone ask me if I know what's going to happen in the next book before I write it. Well, I do to a point. I have certain milestones that I plan on meeting, but for some reason, Jen, Zeke, and the others seem to come up with a way to send the story in a whole other direction.

But that's what makes writing so fun to me. I love letting the characters loose to wreak havoc. Sometimes it ends up as nothing but outtakes from the book, and other times it takes it to a whole new level.

That's why I can't wait to write the next book. I want to see what's going to happen!

If you'd like to keep up with what I've got coming out, sign up for my email list at uprising.marobbins.com. You'll get a **free** eBook, new release announcements, updates, and even some drawings to win prizes like signed paperbacks and other unique items.

Thank you so much for reading the Citadel. Know that I take no reader for granted and I'm truly humbled that you spent your time reading my book.

Till next time.

M.A. Robbins

ACKNOWLEDGMENTS

I couldn't write enough books to give my wife, Debbie, the acknowledgment she deserves. Thanks to Domi at Inspired Cover Designs for her talent, patience, and quick turn-arounds. To Tamara Blain of A Closer Look Editing, who goes beyond the grammar and spelling, and finds other gremlins I've missed. And to the core beta readers who took their time to read the first three books of this series and provide their two cents: Maureen Meyer and Wayne Tripp. Last but not least, I have to acknowledge TBone for ~~his patience~~ not whining too loudly while waiting for me to finish a chapter before I take him outside to play.

ALSO BY M.A. ROBBINS

The Zombie Uprising Series
    The Awakening, Book One
    The Gauntlet, Book Two

The Tilt Series
    The Tilt, Book One

Printed in Great Britain
by Amazon